A BIG WIND FOR SUMMER

Books by Gavin Black

A BIG WIND FOR SUMMER

by Gavin Black

HARP·ER & ROW, PUBLISHERS

New York, Evanston, San Francisco, London

A HARPER NOVEL OF SUSPENSE

FIRST U.S. EDITION

Designed by Sidney Feinberg

Library of Congress Cataloging in Publication Data

Wynd, Oswald, 1913–
  A big wind for summer.
  I. Title.
PZ3.W986Bh3 [PR6073.Y65]   823'.9'14   75–25076
ISBN 0–06–010366–3

76 77 78 79 10 9 8 7 6 5 4 3 2 1

To Jay Weston, for whom the sun always shines in Scotland

ONE

The envelope was addressed in a wobbly hand, and had been forwarded from the offices of the small shipbuilding company on the Clyde which I had just sold to Texas oil interests. The writing inside was even wobblier, but for all that indicated a strong personality, great loops down for the *l*'s and the *y*'s but short on upstrokes, suggesting that the lady had her feet firmly on the earth and was without too much interest in heaven.

> Tigh-na-Claddach
> Isle of Arran
> 17th June

Dear Mr. Harris,

    I apologize for my writing but I am arthritic and hold a pen with some difficulty. I happened quite by chance to see in the *Glasgow Herald* a short item about the sale of a shipyard on the Clyde as part of this dreadful oil business happening all around us, but it was only when Harris and Company of Singapore was mentioned that I realized you must be the son of one of my dearest friends (as also of my late husband, Sir John Martin-Macintosh). At once a great flood of memories came sweeping over me. You will not, probably, remember me or my husband, but he was British Resident in Tetuan (the last before "Freedom") and I certainly remember you. I can see you now in the family house in Singapore, rather a slight boy, at that time somewhat under the shadow of your elder brother, who later died so tragically. I ought to have realized, of course, that after this you became the head of Harris and Company, but I knew nothing of the firm's Scottish interests or that you ever visited this country.

Your father we used to see often, in Malaysia before John became Resident of Tetuan, and later on in that island itself. Your father was our guest for the coronation of the Rajah of Tetuan. I know that John had hopes at one time that your father could be persuaded to establish a branch office of Harris and Company in Tetuan, the island in those days having much more importance than it does now since the discovery of more oil on the mainland of Borneo just beyond it. Oil seems to bring the most unwanted changes everywhere and these days here in Scotland (ten years ago who would have ever dreamed it possible?) we may any of us wake up to see an oil derrick at work beyond us out on what used to be untainted waters.

John's and my life in Malaysia and Tetuan is now so long ago and so much has happened since, including that dreadful war which your dear father didn't survive. (I remember how upset John was when we got the news about that.) The Far East has changed beyond all recognition since the British withdrawal (tragically far too soon) and I find myself just hating to read about what is happening out there these days. Whatever they may say about colonial administration, we did look *after* our people. And who looks after them now? But then I'm just a leftover. The Victorians had a word for it—a Relict. So often that is just what I feel.

By the time you receive this you may be planning to leave Scotland or, in these days of quick flights, be back in Singapore, but should it happen that you are staying on for a short holiday after having completed your business, may I make a suggestion? It may seem an impertinence, but I am asking it in the name of old friendship with your father, and it is that, if it is at all possible, you visit me here in Arran. Alas, it is quite impossible for me to come to Glasgow these days for a meeting between us, as I am a semi-invalid.

Arran is, of course, a famous beauty spot which perhaps, if you haven't seen it, you ought to, and I do wish that I could ask you to stay here, but circumstances at Tigh-na-Claddach make it impossible to offer proper hospitality. The hotels, however, are quite good and you might enjoy your stay in one of them, sparing me an afternoon visit here. My appeal to you is not simply a matter of nostalgia for lost days. I need the help of someone positioned as you are in life, and need it badly. In a way it might be a matter of *life* or *death* for me.

I hope you won't feel that this is a communication from a half-crazed old woman (which *some* might call me) and I cannot tell you how grateful I would be for a visit from you, not to mention advice from someone whose interests lie back in that world which remains the only real one to me.

Yours most sincerely,
Eloise Martin-Macintosh

I poured another cup of coffee, added milk, which turned it mud color, then looked out of the window. It was raining. My hotel was near Loch Lomond but had no view of it, just of trees beyond waterlogged meadows, trees huge after a hundred years of well-soaked roots. With a bit more sun they could have made the framework for the tangle of jungle. Traffic hissed on a road becoming crowded with tourist cars, their roofs just visible beyond a hedge, regular fountains of spray shooting up from tire impact with undrained water. I had meant soon to be adding to that clutter on the highways, heading my rented Hillman Avenger north toward Ullapool, with a booking for it on the next day's ferry to Stornoway in the Outer Hebrides.

The weather reports were dismal. A deep depression centered over the North Atlantic was moving toward Scotland to take the place of another depression which had just left for Norway. It was one of those summers in Britain when a tropical resident can really count on getting the prescribed change from equatorial sun which is supposed to do him a world of good, but so far the treatment had only left me feeling slightly depressed.

I read the letter again, with special emphasis on those under-lined references to life or death. What could Lady Martin-Macintosh mean? She had to be of an age when death was practically right ahead on schedule anyway, and the old ought to have the thought of this sharing their rooms, accepting the facts with a certain graciousness if they still value their own identities. That "Relict" was capitalized, suggesting self-pity. I didn't much care, either, for the bit about looking after the natives, the concept that colonialism had been basically paternal. I don't deny that a minority of its servants worked with dedication for the people among whom they lived, but my family hadn't belonged to that group. The Harrises had been dedicated to making money for themselves as fast as possible and buying the good life with it, including nine indoor servants in our Singapore house and four outdoor. These days I make my own breakfast in three rooms, but I'm not sure that basic motivation has changed much. I'm out East still because I'm uneasy away from it for long, but if things get too bad for Westerners in the area I have the money to run for it to the south of France and probably will.

I went up to my room to pack for the Outer Hebrides, mostly woolen sweaters. I was going out to the Atlantic islands because they are what the Harris family left when they invaded the outer world and I have always been curious about the life we abandoned. Was there peace out there? If we had stayed spinning tweeds on our crofts, plus lugging seaweed up to fertilize fifteen acres of stony soil, with bagpipes and Calvinism for recreation, would we have been nearer to whole men, supported into our eighties by honest, if toil-haggard, women? Or would the Harrises now be potential psychopaths from ingrowing boredom? I didn't know. I was going to try to find out.

"A matter of *life* or *death* for me." Damn and blast the woman!

There were no phones in the bedrooms and I went down to the reception counter, pinging the bell.

"Hello, there," said the quite pretty student from inner London on summer work.

"I want to find out the best way to get to Arran."

"Never heard of it." She smiled. "I'll ask the manager."

You get to Arran via the most unattractive industrial areas Scotland has produced and then across Ayrshire, which didn't attract me too much either. It looks a little like a wet Ohio: for corn as high as an elephant's eye read wheat up to thigh level; the same huge cars belonging to rich farmers, the same small towns where they do most of their shopping, and no hint of big water at all even though in this case it is only just over the horizon. I was making for the port of Ardrossan and reached it through a tangle of overgrown villages on the coast, these once the resorts that poor Scots went to for their holidays but now, richer, appear to have abandoned, the stone boardinghouses desolate, the parks haunted by music from yesterday's bands. Here generations of potential emigrants made sand castles on the now half-polluted beaches, and no doubt in New Zealand and Australia and Canada the names of these places still strike chords of nostalgia among elderly expatriates, but in the rain they just looked utterly unloved and without hope, fodder for bulldozers.

In the dockyard area I stopped the car by a man who was working away digging up pavings with a pick, a squad of one assigned the lifetime task of getting rid of Ardrossan as a port. He leaned on a handle while water ran unnoticed down his nose, a deserter from the Highlands, slow-voiced.

"It iss the Arran boat you are wanting, then? Aye, well, it iss over there. First right, then left, then right again. After that you will be following the railway tracks. Mind, you'll never be getting the weather for the islands."

I could see that. I thanked him and drove on, wipers hissing, beginning to feel a certain affection for the Avenger. Any car that could stand up to these conditions and still keep ticking must be built north of the border. The Swedes construct their transport to contend with ice and snow; the Scots, like Noah, to defeat damp. And so far there hadn't been a trickle anywhere inside, which is more than I could say for the last luxury job I had owned when it was subjected to the tropic downpour test.

The Arran ferry was a mini-liner, all white paintwork and streamlining, with huge areas of glass upperwork and a yawning mouth in her stern. I got out inside a vast clanging cave and went through a hatch for the stairs to the passenger decks, making for the dining saloon, in which I found out it had been a mistake to plan on lunching aboard, the menu having been built around the national dish, fish and soggy chips. We sailed into a grayness broken by whitecapped waves too noticeable through those plate-glass windows, visibility reaching to about five miles, where it was stopped by a cloud bank resting on the water. I got the impression there was no land immediately ahead, that we were bound for New York on a ship that mightn't stand up too well to the crossing.

Rolling began; not bad, just enough to make four or five people decide against the meal they had ordered, and when I moved to the lounge quite a number in there were looking uneasy, too. There was a decidedly unhappy dog, a large Alsatian used to keeping up a bold front, but now demoralized, sitting on the floor swaying back and forth, with his tongue out. I tried the decks, but they were too wet for parading, so I went back to a plastic sofa and unfolded the day's copy of the paper that had betrayed me to Lady Eloise.

There was an article on Singapore, which surprised me on two counts: first that it was there at all, British journalism in both press and television currently showing a marked tendency toward devoted navel-watching; the second reason being that I couldn't disagree with the foreign correspondent's conclusions. Something odd happened as I read, black print on white turning to black print on pale yellow. I turned my head. Halfway on the sixteen-mile crossing we had suddenly moved into a gap between two depressions. The ferry was in sunshine.

I couldn't see the gap lasting for long and went out on deck to enjoy it, the sun real, becoming red enough to raise steam from planking. Dead ahead, at about five miles, was the island of Arran, pushing up from the sea under a Caribbean-blue sky in which there were a few flecks of innocent white cloud, the softened pyramid of the chief mountain, Goat Fell, needing only a wisp of smoke drifting from the peak to be an active volcano, its slopes a polished, lustrous green. To the north was another group of mountains, these without a hint of glacial smoothing: spiked, torn black rock like lava, the jagged remnants from some vast eruption.

I put my hands on the rail and leaned forward, knowing suddenly that it wasn't Lady Eloise who had brought me here, but that practiced whore again who always, when I am about to leave her in a sudden lust for sun, does this to me and, with a kind of laughter, says that tropic-born I may be, but I am in thrall here, too. I don't keep coming back to any business on the Clyde, but from a recurring need for what is in the blood and can't be denied, for a big ration of the damp and a little ration of what lies between two major meteorological disturbances.

Penang is not the most beautiful island in the world; Arran is —at times—and so is Islay, and Mull and Barra, even Skye of the tourists and the strict Presbyterians. The sun comes briefly in Scotland to devalue all static warm loveliness, to make that the ordinary of daily habit, somehow almost mean against the occasional eighteen-carat gift in this northern place.

We came into Brodick with a flourish of frothing propellers, like a cruise liner approaching Bali, the heat of the sun confirmed now, and the air turned so soft that when I got to the car I shed one sweater. The forward ramp clanged down and even above the rumbling of a truck's diesel I heard the screaming of sea gulls, as I drove out onto a long pier which offered a good view of the little capital, a crescent of hotels, but all spaced, set well back in gardens, none of them tower blocks. I decided to leave someplace to stay until later and took the first road to the left outside the dock area, climbing under green shade to high ground on which were contemporary villas decently surrounded by a third of an acre, new homes offering staggering vistas of island and estuary and the distant mainland for those who had the thirty thousand pounds plus to pay for one of them. There was money on Arran, the kind of money that can buy landscaped surrounds screening paved patios. You don't get a mountain that should have been a volcano in your view these days if you're running a chronic overdraft, and Brodick was sleek with fat credit balances.

The road belonged to Volvos and Jaguars—and a Ford Popular towing a trailer, the driver looking unhappy as I passed him, as though already he was wondering where he could find a campsite for the night in restricted territory. The woods were immaculate, regimented rows of larch and spruce sweeping back from tarmac, wire-fenced to keep out deer and tourists. I was beginning to get the feeling that, if it had been caught in time, the island might have been kept as a reservation for the very rich and probably many of the residents wish it had been, that the annual influx of holidaymakers could be turned off at source. I saw Lamlash and braked to a stop.

The car was about four hundred feet up, the road ahead a serpentine drop, flanked by a golf course defying the gradient, to a deepwater bay sheltered by a strategically placed hilly little island. There were wide beaches and a scatter of white houses and in the safe anchorage dozens of boats, some moored, some under sail. A large yacht, certainly from the south, swung arrogant on her anchor chain, at least a hundred-and-twenty-footer, with a gangplank lowered and a mahogany power launch tethered alongside. Lamlash gave no hint at all of a Britain once again with her back to an economic wall; it could be because the escapers from a harsh reality had moved here, likely to be safe enough as long as those banks in Zurich stayed solvent.

I spent the afternoon in raw tourism varied by stops at hotels to ask if they had a room for me. None of them did and eventually I headed back toward Brodick from the south end of the island, through a glen completely empty of houses and people. I met few cars and didn't even see many sheep, but on a number of telephone poles a poster was being eliminated by wind and weather. At one that was intact I got out to have a look: a large photograph of an Oriental wearing a dhoti and sitting in the Buddha-on-lotus-leaf position. Very big black letters identified the gentleman as Swami Gundarajati and beneath the picture were the words, in red: "The New Enlightenment." If there is anyplace for commercialized Eastern mysticism, it certainly isn't a Scottish island. I ripped the thing down, stopping twice more to continue this missionary work.

It was half past six by the time I got back to Brodick, wanting a bath, a long drink, and food, prepared to pay heavily for all three. The top hotel offered crystal chandeliers and an English deb putting in time as a receptionist until she could get back to Switzerland for the skiing. Her smile was without pity. They were booked up until October and she rather implied by a class of people who didn't drive up in Hillman Avengers, there being nothing cheaper than BMWs out in the parking lot. I tried two more hotels in my guide and three that weren't, all catering to economy-car owners, but they hadn't rooms until October either. At the boardinghouses they were in the middle of serving fish high teas and I was stared at through bow windows by elderly couples who stopped chewing, as though I was some kind of threat to their security. All of half a dozen little maids imported for the season from the Outer Hebrides came perspiring from noisy kitchens to tell me that I hadn't a hope of a bed or anything to eat either.

The Scottish summer sun was still shining brightly, but Brodick was beginning to lose its appeal. There was no point in trying one of those villas up on the hill for bed and breakfast; they'd set their wolfhounds onto me. I went up to a policeman outside an ice cream shop. He was a pleasant-spoken man, but not really very helpful, passing on a problem to colleagues by suggesting that I try Lamlash or Whiting Bay.

"I've been to both. No rooms. What do I do if I can't get in anyplace?"

9

"Aye, I wonder."

"What about farmhouses?"

"Well, you find that people come back to them every year. They're not great for strangers."

"Look, first things first. How about a restaurant?"

"It'll be shut now. They only do high teas, early."

I went into the ice cream shop, where the Italian behind the counter looked like a contented millionaire, and bought a large bar of milk chocolate, a can of Coca-Cola, two packets of biscuits, plus some fruit, emerging just as the ferry tooted an invitation to join it on the last trip of the day back to the mainland. But I was damned if I was going. I had been summoned to this island by a Lady once the wife of the ruler of another island ten times the size of Arran, and if the worst came to the worst I'd ring her up with a demand for Far Eastern hospitality.

I got back into the car which could turn out to be my only shelter from a Highland night, glad that I had paid more for the deluxe model with tip-back front seats, and was gnawing on a piece of chocolate when it came to me that I hadn't really been serious about looking for accommodation in Lamlash, which might be worth trying again.

The view from the top of the hill didn't stop my breath the second time around. The two hotels were serving dinner, one stewing their steak in a rich gravy, the other frying it with onions, both setting my gastric juices flowing, but I got no change—near rudeness from one reception desk and the helpful suggestion from the other that I try Whiting Bay, but that I would be too late for any food anywhere. I took irritation that was moving toward rage out on the little car, slamming the driver's door, which was unkind. We set off farther south, white houses and luxury yachts well to the rear, when suddenly the road was shadowed from evening sun by a mass of towering trees behind a stone wall. Below the high growth was another security screen of rhododendrons. There was a gate in the wall, swung back, with rusted iron grillwork and more rhododen-

10

drons growing through it so thickly that I almost missed the sign. It was brown and weathered, with only one word still faintly visible: "Hotel."

My reaction was instinctive. I jerked the car around without signaling. The drive reminded me of a jungle *rentis,* one of those tracks cut into rain forest which can be traversed on four wheels if you are adventurous and not afraid of tigers. There were potholes full of water. The Avenger bounced and groaned, not liking this, but I pressed on, seeing daylight ahead, forcing the car up to seven miles an hour, and was rewarded suddenly by a clearing.

This had once been lawn. Now it was eligible for the cultivation of hay, with, beyond, the perfect pile for the setting of a Gothic novel in which the young heroine is slowly being done to death by a sadistic stepfather. For years she has been trying to escape, but always before she gets to the gate the terrible hired man comes out of the bushes and grabs her.

It was an enormous Victorian edifice built as a holiday palace back in the days when one percent of the British population had all the money. Democracy, plus successive Labour governments, have made assorted newcomers rich but have eliminated that essential for the maintenance of large establishments —plenty of servants. It was a long time since this house had been properly staffed or been subjected to a week's work from painters, but it was still lived in; one parked Land-Rover proved this. I circled what had once been an ornamental rockery and slid in alongside the other vehicle, switching off the engine but suddenly almost reluctant to step out of security. When I did it was to face a frontage ruled over by twin sets of huge bay windows rising for two stories and topped off by wooden gingerbread work at the eaves, most of which had dropped off. Between the bays was a front door, closed, but a French window was open into what must have been the grand drawing room. Three stone steps led up to this entrance.

The room beyond was enormous, with a heavy, ornate plaster

ceiling, but furnished like the village hall for a whist drive, sets of card tables down two walls with folding chairs tucked into them, each equipped with one ashtray on the green baize. At the far end everything went wildly modern, a chromium, plastic, and Formicaed bar with racks of bottles behind and one pinky light on. There were three people in the room, a barman and two customers. One of the customers, in tweeds and a deerstalker that he wore though indoors, had his foot up on a rail and one hand around a pewter mug. The second customer, a depressed-looking character in a raincoat, was sitting at a card table two down from the bar. All three were looking at me.

The impressive thing then was the utter silence; the birds outside had already gone to bed and though there was a door open onto a dark hall, not a sound came that would hint of activity in the building. There was no smell of food cooking either, just a rumor of disinfectant used in the morning's swab of bare floorboards. My feet made a lot of noise as I walked forward.

"I'm looking for a room for the night."

The barman picked up a glass. His voice was English, with more than a splash of cockney.

"We're full up."

I don't mind being lied to, but I like the lies to have at least a fringe of credibility, as a matter of courtesy. From what I had seen of roofs bulging back from that bay-windowed frontage, this place ought to have at least twenty bedrooms, and if these were in use, or their occupants in the process of being fed, there would be sounds coming from somewhere. I stood there listening, watched by three sets of eyes.

"I'll pay in advance," I said.

This is a formula that works well in third-class establishments out East. It didn't here.

"You heard me," the barman said.

He was two-thirds bald, with a slightly simian face under that extended forehead, and highly colored, almost red. The man in the deerstalker was highly colored, too, in his case the tones purplish. He lifted the tankard, emptied it, set it down on the bar and then said in a loud and echoing voice:

"Make it a stengah this time, George."

I wasn't on Arran, I was in Somerset Maugham country. When I was a boy in Malaysia a whisky and soda was called a stengah. It hasn't been for twenty-five years. I went close to the bar.

"A stengah for me, too," I said.

For seconds there was something very near to that heavy tropic night silence that ought to have been torn apart by the eerie cry of a hunting black panther, but it was deerstalker who broke it.

"You *know* what you're ordering?"

"Sure."

"Where the hell are you from?"

"Singapore."

"Good Lord! Ever go to Kuala Lumpur?"

"I have an office there. I'm up at least every month."

"K.L.! Good old K.L.! You on home leave?"

"Some might call it that."

"Just touring about and you came in here?"

"That's it."

"George! Did you hear that?"

George, now polishing the glass, was not interested.

"Why come to Arran?" deerstalker shouted.

"Just a piece of rubbernecking tourism."

"I see. Look, the name's Henderson-Pratt. Ex-Indian Army. Ex-Malay Regiment. Major. I used to spend half my life in the old Dog in K.L. How is it?"

"Still there."

"Best club in the world. Saturday nights still what they used to be?"

"Maybe not quite."

"God, they were marvelous. Sometimes I think about it. . . . Who are you, anyway?"

"The name is Harris."

"Can't quite place it. Odd we never met out there."

That didn't seem so odd to me. The world that had been Major Henderson-Pratt's in Malaysia had never been mine.

"I say, George, you can find a room for Harris, can't you?"

"We don't take people now, Major. You know that."

"I know, but this is different. I mean you can't send this chap out into the night. Been trying other places, have you, Harris?"

"Everywhere. No rooms, no meals."

"We don't do meals either," George said.

"Oh, balls! They do the most splendid curry you ever tasted in your life. Outside of home territory, that is. The real stuff, too. Turmeric, saffron. All freshly ground. *You* know."

"*No*, Major!"

"Now look here, George. You've got a license in this place and you're supposed to run a hotel. I don't want to put the screw on, but I could. One word in the ear of the county councillor and, well, you'd be for the soup. I know your reasons for not letting rooms and all that, but Harris is from the East, he'll understand—"

Something in George's expression made the major bite off what he had been going to say. Two stengahs were prepared in silence and I bought increased affability from deerstalker by paying for both.

"Are you staying on the island for a bit?"

"I may, if I like it."

"Oh, you're bound to . . . if you get the weather. Bloody sun needs to shine a bit more. Otherwise, fine, you know."

Something in his tone qualified that.

"You must come and meet the wife, Harris. Have a meal one night. She's not much of a cook, I'm afraid. Didn't have to out East. Staff, and all that. She's never really got used to not having 'em. Bit hard on her, really. I mean coming home. Bit hard on me, too, actually."

He laughed.

"I'd be grateful for something to eat," I said.

The major glared at George. "You hear that? This man's hungry. You can't say no. How about letting me have a word with your missus?"

A voice said, "You want to speak to me, Major?"

A girl stood in the doorway to the hall. She was wearing a sheath dress made from a sarong print, the effect rather spoiled by a fluffy wool cardigan. Even in a poor light I was at once certain she was a Malay-Chinese mix, one of the successful mixes. She was very near to being beautiful.

TWO

The major phoned a wife who couldn't cook, and stayed for curry. His life work had been training other people to do without him, first in the British Army of India, then, when that faded, attached to a Malay regiment, supervising weapon training and square bashing. There had been no chance of promotion to colonel; he had spent twenty years on the way out, not up. When everything out East finally closed down on him, he and his wife had retired to the south of England, but soon finding that far too expensive for his pension, were driven north by inflation to land in a small croft house on Arran. Here, too, he had missed his chance, turning down an offer in 1970 for five times what he had paid for the property. Now it was improbable that he could give it away.

"But where could we have gone if we had sold, Harris? Rents are impossible, and there's no hope of our sort getting on any public housing list up here."

"Why not?"

"We're foreigners, old boy. And the Scots don't like us. Damn noticeable these days, too. Out here they're saying we've done the locals out of their homes. Islanders who sold ten years ago can't forget the prices they might have got seven or eight years later. Makes them sour. Highlanders are as greedy as hell."

There was a slight rising of the hackles on the back of my neck, but three whiskies on an empty stomach had somewhat anaesthetized the fiery Harris temperament and I didn't reach for one of the table knives to use as a dirk. We were in an empty dining room, better furnished than the bar across the hall, but not much; our table was in the bay window, with a view of that hayfield. There hadn't been glowing coals in the fireplace for at least a quarter of a century and the room had that bone-reaching chill which is supposed to be the right climate for ghosts. I wasn't afraid of the supernatural, just pneumonia. Previous visits to the ancestral homeland enabled me to identify the smell that went with the cold: dry rot, busily destroying the main fabric of the building.

The major was suffering from a bad case of nostalgia for what he had never been. If he had taken time to consider this, he should have realized that I was quite the worst possible audience for his fictions, since I couldn't believe any of them. Colonialism rushing toward its inevitable end had seen a thousand Major Henderson-Pratts stranded like jellyfish by the high tide of change, pathetic figures desperately trying to prop up their corners of a dying world from which the more alert and the more intelligent had long since departed. You saw them in decaying sahib's clubs breaking the old no-hard-liquor-before-sundown rule with gins at midday, loud-voiced in a bid to make one man's noise fill an emptiness that should have been peopled by fifty.

We sat with elbows on a dubious cloth, the fourth whisky in front of us, waiting for food. At least, I was waiting for it; the major was quite pleased to babble on: Kuala Lumpur, Ipoh, the races, Tanglin, absolutely splendid beach parties at Morib, and the time he had gone on a tiger shoot. I was dreading his backpace from Malaysia to the old days in India and to stave this off broke through the monologue with a query about the girl who was presumably hard at it preparing our curry. She was, as I had

17

guessed, Sino-Malay, with a name favored by princesses—Aishah. Her background, however, didn't rate any of the major's fictions; neither did George's. The barman, who was soon going to double as our waiter, had finished a short service army engagement as a sergeant, from which he had joined the colonial police, also as a sergeant, a rank which didn't allow him into any of the major's clubs or to join tiger shoots. George had met Aishah at one of Singapore's "Worlds," where she was a dance hostess. The major was damn sure—whispering—that she hadn't lost her virginity to George, and she had been fourteen when he met her. She was over thirty now and still no fading tropic flower.

When the Singapore police became Orientalized, George moved to Hong Kong, where colonialism remained stable, leaving Aishah behind, back on her job, with overtime, at the "World." Then quite suddenly he had come south on leave and married the girl. His bosses in Hong Kong had not approved. George got out of the police and came back to Britain, with Aishah, working first as a barman, then getting into the catering trade via an eatery on a motorway.

"After that they came here," the major said, still in a hissing whisper. "They got this place damn cheap. No one else wanted it."

"How long ago was that?"

"It must be eight years. It's twelve since George left Hong Kong."

The tropic flower had been preserved in Scottish deep freeze; in Singapore she would have been running to fat, middle-aged.

"Why no guests here?"

In spite of the whisky, discretion clamped down on the major. George out East was legitimate gossip material, but George on Arran was the proprietor of the local club for ex-colonials.

"Bit of trouble," was all he said, then stood. "Look, old boy, let me pop through to the bar and get you another whisky?"

"Beer. A half pint."

He seemed relieved. While the major was absent, a door at the far end of the long room opened and George came in, carrying a laden tray. There were beads of sweat on his forehead, and his high color was even higher. He set dishes on the table, breathing heavily. As a guest taken in under pressure, I felt I had to say something.

"This smells wonderful. Where do you get the stuff for a curry on Arran?"

A tureen of rice was set down as a centerpiece and I thought I wasn't going to get an answer, but one came, explosive.

"London. By post. Vegetables from Glasgow. Bloody islanders won't grow 'em. Too damn lazy. Like Malays."

The major came back with half pints and was loudly amiable, but George knew we had been talking about him and hated us for it. The curry was not really a gastronomic experience but still quite an achievement in the circumstances, and only an Oriental could have cooked that rice. While we ate, other cars braved the driveway and voices came from the bar against a background of pop music switched on. After eating we went back to where life was happening. About a dozen men were standing about, which still didn't give that ex-drawing room a cozy feel. The native islander in the raincoat, if he had been that, was now gone and none of the newcomers had the soft voices of Highlanders, or the rougher ones of mainland Scots either, for that matter. I was introduced to a former tea planter from Assam, a noisy extrovert, and an ex-Indian civil servant who was as introverted as they come. He had been forcibly retired from his job a quarter of a century ago, a man with sad faded blue eyes which he could nonetheless glue onto you as though he knew his only hope of holding an audience was by hypnosis. I missed his name somehow but was still forced to take that life story of a quarter of a century's inactivity, the first phase of this having been passed in the Seychelles Islands, to which he had moved, with his tiny pension, because it was the cheapest place in an expensive world.

"Why did you leave?" I asked.

"My God, haven't you heard what they've done to the Seychelles? It used to be heaven. The only way you could get there was five days on the old *Kampala* from Bombay. She called every six weeks with a handful of people and supplies. You know what we used to pay for whisky?"

He told me what they had paid for whisky, and gin, the real luxury being powdered milk, which you could do without in paradise. He had really loved those islands, which General Gordon, who lost his head in Khartoum, decided were the original Garden of Eden, a garden totally overlooked by Satan since that unfortunate snake episode. But the devil had come back suddenly via a landing place for jumbo jets, creating an anteroom to hell. The retiree kept spraying my face with his fury as he told me about it. The only reason he was now on Arran was that he had been able to sell his slice of heaven to a development syndicate for a price which allowed him to face up to British inflation, but not Seychellian. He had come home looking for another island, but I didn't get the impression that he thought the Arran palms a good substitute for the Indian Ocean species.

All the time I stood there enduring this lament, another bar patron kept staring at me. He was leaning against a wall drinking beer, antisocial, not talking to anyone. I had a feeling I had seen his face before and he certainly seemed to know mine. He was in his thirties somewhere, running a bit to weight, but obviously once a dedicated athlete, broad-shouldered, with a head that ten years ago would have been handsome and was still only slightly damaged by jowl sag. Black curly hair was receding a bit, but the process had only just started. I broke through hypnosis and moved over.

"Where did we last meet?"

He answered at once. "Kuala Lumpur."

"That still doesn't give me your name."

"Why should it? I partnered you in a golf foursome."

"Then I know why you remember me. My golf's still terrible."

"I remember you because you're Paul Harris."

At our one meeting this man had decided he didn't like me.

"You'd just become a Malaysian subject," he said. "Everyone was talking about it."

"That wasn't my fault."

"Wasn't it? You mean you didn't give what you were doing full publicity? I'll bet you hired a press agent to announce it. Like an actor who's just had a vasectomy."

Our contact was moving out of neutral. I stood smiling at him. He wasn't smiling back.

"It's paid off, hasn't it?" he asked. "Becoming a native?"

"In some ways. What's your two handicap done for you?"

He showed me white teeth then. "Good guess. It was two in Malaysia. It's four now."

"Who were you working for in K.L.?"

"Huntley and Greig. They sacked me."

That dealt with his business career in the Orient. Huntley and Greig are a long-established importer-exporter firm who seem to me to have handicapped themselves by sticking to the old British commercial principle that a low golf handicap is likely to mean top executive potential, a business philosophy I have always been highly suspicious of myself. However, H. and G. are practical about their application of this theory: they bring out about twice as many low-handicap men as they estimate they'll need over the years, in due course shipping home more than half of them, and with a very small golden handshake.

"My name's Angus Kennet. Not that it'll mean anything to you."

He was right, it didn't, surprising because I usually have total recall of what I have done to golf partners.

"Maybe Ma-in-law will mean more. From the big time out there. Lady Martin-Macintosh."

"Oh," I said, cautious.

"I take it you remember the old bitch?"

"I think I do. Is she still alive?"

"She'll be alive in the year two thousand. At a hundred and twenty the last surviving British Resident's widow."

"Living in England?"

"No. Right here." He was bitter.

"You've got quite a colony of ex-colonials."

"Sure. It's getting worse than Spain. A couple establish themselves, then suck in their old Far Eastern pals. Like a breeder reactor, explosive expansion. The real islanders are thinking of petitioning the government to stop immigration. How long are you here for?"

"A few days. I'm a tourist."

"Don't tell me someone recommended this place?"

"Nowhere else would give me a bed."

"What did I tell you? The natives are starting to fight back."

The major came up.

"Hello, Angus. How about a game sometime?"

"All right. Only not on the Lamlash course. I'm a golfer, not a mountain goat. Make it Brodick. Give me a ring."

Kennet put down his empty glass, gave a nod toward us both, then walked down the room.

"Funny sort of chap," the major said. "Wasn't a success out East. Chip on his shoulder, that sort of thing. Good golfer, though."

The major wanted to switch back from beer to whisky, so I bought him one.

"What's Lady Martin-Macintosh like?" I asked.

"Thinks she's the first cousin of the Almighty. We don't rate there."

Social advances by the Henderson-Pratts had been repelled by a former Resident's Relict. It was weird in the converted drawing room of a moldering old Scottish mansion house to come smack up against midcentury colonial social stratification.

In British Malaya the Army was always two levels down from the ruling elite; you had your local military commander and his wife to dinner once a year as a matter of decency, but would never dream of asking them to the residency for informal bridge.

A picture of Eloise Martin-Macintosh was building up. I could see her coming down the steps from a terrace at the Tetuan annual garden party, doing this exactly as she had observed the Queen doing it at Buckingham Palace, the Resident's lady facing rather a different crowd, of course, turbans and bright silks down there waiting, while she herself was in floppy voile under an enormous hat to protect a British complexion from the dreadful tropic sun. A band would be playing; Sir John would have trained one, an odd mix of percussion and gamelan sending its strange noise out from the shade of a flame-of-the-forest tree. No alcohol would be served, just fruit juices and ices, Sir John himself having been well fortified before he left the library.

It all felt like the established order a hundred years ago, yet I had seen it myself, dragged to the most dismal of ceremonials by my father, who was very conscious of the position he had to keep up in the community. Father must certainly have enjoyed the coronation of the Rajah of Tetuan, decidedly his thing, ten days of pomp and circumstance topped off by long formal dinners under flapping punkahs, the ladies in damp corsets, the gentlemen with dark patches under the arms of their tunics. Even the conversation was prescribed; you never mentioned anything nasty, like real life.

When I announced that I was going to my room, the major said:

"I hope your bed isn't damp. Rheumatism's hell out here."

The bed *was* damp. A hot-water bottle created an area of high humidity in the middle of the mattress, this almost steaming. I had a choice between the torrid zone and dank pajamas or keeping back in the permafrost. I chose warmth, risking lumbago, trying to get to sleep by my usual formula, sedative thought about the only house I have really cared for, which burned down. It was on its own hill in Kuala Lumpur and at three every morning the wind from the Strait of Malacca used to come whispering along the verandas, setting old wood to creaking. Almost every dawn a golden oriole sang in one of the carefully preserved hardwood trees.

I didn't manage to evoke that oriole before I slept, just woke to the noise of sparrows, a whole congress of them. Something had happened to knock that threatening second depression off course and my window was a white square promising to go yellow before long. All the Lamlash sparrows used these trees and it sounded as though the Whiting Bay ones had moved along to join them for a special morning service to fine weather. It was 4 A.M. and I was hungry.

A trip to the bathroom took a bit of thinking about. I had to go out into a once grand upper hall now badly in need of redecorating, with walls that seemed to be bending inward under the weight of vast, gilt-framed, time-dulled etchings of Highland beasts. After this it was down stairs to a half landing and then up another flight into a corridor which had no lighting of any kind; you guessed the position of the door you wanted. I had oriented myself pretty well the night before and guessed right, opening into a minor aesthetic experience, outsize Victorian plumbing on which little rosebuds bloomed everywhere, even inside the bowl of the water closet. The bathroom itself was frigid and the hot tap a liar.

I was coming out again when I heard muffled voices from somewhere up the dark passage, words at first inaudible, then two reaching me very clearly indeed on a woman's shout.

"Anjing busok!"

It could only be Aishah to her husband. Who else in this hotel was likely to be able to appreciate being called, in Malay, a decaying pig?

I drove over potholes with one hand, eating biscuits, turned right at the gate and then quickly right again into a second-class road that became acutely third-class as it started to climb. At the top of a glen I parked, ate a banana, then got out and walked over new heather toward a modest summit, reaching this before sunup.

The view was impressive. To the east, and nearly twenty miles away, that part of Scotland which works was shrouded under industrial smog. Westward the long, low peninsula of Kintyre was under clear skies, white farmhouses shining out. Beyond Kintyre and a good deal of open sea was the shape of Islay, a big island which starts a pattern of these, all of them fragments torn from the mainland by glacial ice, most of their hills honed down into a sensual smoothness, two the first thing that sailors see coming in from the Atlantic, the paps of Jura. But I couldn't see them; they were still wearing a cloud bra. It is all a fairly large area, mainly inhabited by people who believe that work was the devil's invention and you serve the Lord best by avoiding it whenever possible. Out here men were still in their beds, leaving all activity to sheep and cattle, and these weren't moving about much. Sixty miles to the south, Belfast might be emerging from more night bombings, but such violence was unthinkable on Arran, a windless stillness in which the sudden cry of a grouse traveled for miles over peat bog.

Sun came up over Scotland as dramatically as the sun Kipling attributed to Burma, only he was stretching poetic license a bit: there is no bay on the road to Mandalay, and no China near there either. Here the thunder was suddenly provided by a jumbo jet en route from Prestwick to New York, one of those explosions across deep peace to remind us that there aren't any nirvanas left, all silences, even polar ones, being under permanent threat. I looked up at ribbons of exhaust pollution and remembered that this island had been on Concorde's trial route down the British Isles, during which exercise the plane had shattered the windows of remote houses and driven farm collies mad. Color came, remarkable blues on the water, forty tones of green on the land, but nature-worship was over and on my way back to the car there were two more jets, one in from the direction of Montreal, the other out, probably making for Detroit with a quota of electronics executives returning to the head office for top-level consultations on the running of their Scottish factories. The sheep had got used to the recurring din; not a head was raised toward the heavens from grass-munching.

George served me my breakfast, the conventional meal—bacon and eggs, toast, marmalade, tea or coffee, and if you're wise you take tea. I had said good morning, but he had said nothing at all, a man with problems for which he blamed the world, not himself. A phone rang for some time in the hall before it was answered and then George, from around the edge of a door, said:

"For you."

He didn't seem surprised. I was.

The instrument was highly contemporary and lemon-colored, installed as part of the modernization scheme that had been soon abandoned.

"Paul Harris here."

I got a voice that could have belonged to a British actress trained in those days when you were expected to project your lines all the way to the back of the gallery over the rattle of matinee teacups.

"So you've *come!*"

Lady Eloise, without a doubt.

"Your son-in-law told you I was here?"

"No, he did *not.* I have no contact with that person."

Nice household if they all lived together. The lady paused to let me savor what she had said and how she had said it, then went on:

"Anne told me. My daughter."

Anne was liaison officer. I think that if it hadn't been such nice weather, I would then have decided to catch the midday boat back to the mainland, but maybe not; curiosity is my major vice.

"*When* can you come here, Mr. Harris?"

"Almost anytime."

"Ah! Let me think. *This* morning?"

"Why not?"

A pause.

"I don't want anyone to know about your visit. That's extremely important."

It might be to her; it wasn't to me. If security mattered so much, I ought perhaps to suggest that this could already have been breached. George, for all his personal troubles, almost certainly knew who had called me. On a small island he would have heard that voice before. Even on quite big islands the permanent residents all identify each other sooner or later, and Lady Eloise's splendid diphthongs sounding out in a chemist's or grocer's would be as memorable as the voice of the British Broadcasting Corporation's top poetry reader.

"If you came about eleven, Mr. Harris, Anne should be just leaving to shop in Brodick. This is her day."

I got my instructions, which were to drive some fifteen miles to North Sannox, where the Martin-Macintosh house was situated, but not approach it, tucking my car down a little track which led to a sandy beach, waiting there in hiding until a green Mini came by headed south, with Anne in it, plus a large dog. After that I was to walk to Tigh-na-Claddach, which was beyond the next bend in the road, using the drive but passing the main house to a path through a rose bed leading onto a lawn. From the lawn I would see the cottage Lady Eloise had built for herself, where she would be waiting. There was no mention of Angus Kennet as a security problem. By this time my ka, or astral other body, had taken quite firm shape and was standing three feet off shaking its head at me, but I paid no attention and went out into sunlight, to which kas are allergic.

The drive up the east coast was very beautiful, the first part of it completely dominated by Goat Fell. I had to pass through Brodick again, where the luxury hotel which had refused me was now taking a package tour of about forty holidaymakers, complete with bus just unloaded off the ferry. Beyond the town was the castle which some centuries ago acquired the island's best site and then proceeded to screen itself away from the world by a vast plantation of trees, these edging the road, which meant that my only view was east, to the waters of the Firth of Clyde.

There was a lot to see out there: the sister island of Bute, with glistening beaches, and between it and the mainland more small islands, innocent-looking and bright green, but I knew they concealed a mass of electronic devices to protect the U.S. Polaris base farther up the estuary. The channel has almost more traffic these days under the water than on top of it, but what the eye doesn't see the mind doesn't worry about too much, and residents in these parts have grown used to living within a prime target area for Soviet missiles.

Lady Eloise's instructions had been explicit and by half past ten I had reached that little track which led to a sandy beach through a copse of silver birch. I parked the Avenger, got out, and was at once threatened by mountains. These, the by-product of an eruption, I had seen from the ferry, two sets of enormous broken black teeth, with a glen making a deep cleft between. My road map said that the maximum height up there was three thousand feet, but this was straight up from sea level with nothing to give perspective. Trees ran out of enough soil not very far from the road and even grass packed it in as the gradients became perpendicular. I could see no sheep; it wasn't even goat territory, jagged spires offering no hospitality to any-thing, except perhaps rock climbers with a death wish. At higher levels sun was pulling steam out of deep crevices, mak-ing saw-edged pinnacles appear to smoke. Enormous boulders were perched halfway down earlier slides, looking ready to take off again. At the top of the glen a vast rock buttress put a sharp end to sunlight, promising nothing but gloom beyond. Even on a bright day these mountains were sinister; under rain and wind they would give me the horrors.

A green Mini passed at ten minutes to eleven. I couldn't see who was driving because of a vast head shoved out of the window on my side, the world's largest canine suitable for security duties, a bull mastiff with its tongue hanging out. As a breed I don't really care for them. For one thing, they weigh too much for effective owner control; for another, they can be charming one day, when you've been properly introduced, and the next forget all about that formality, proceeding with a bid to tear off one of your legs. It was considerate of Lady Eloise to arrange for the dog to be out when I called.

Tigh-na-Claddach was only a short walk. About forty years earlier, the people who then lived here had done the next best thing to clearing out, putting a screen between themselves and those terrible mountains, a huge plantation of spruce. The trees were carefully maintained, too, surrounded by new deer netting and a barred gate to the drive with wire mesh all over it, presumably to keep the mastiff from attacking passing tourists. There were two notices, one asking me to shut the gate, the other warning about the dog. Postmen must have hated the place.

The drive was overshadowed and rather gloomy. I had been expecting a somewhat gaunt Scots stone house at the end of it, but came around shrubbery onto English cozy, circa 1935 or thereabouts, mullioned windows and all. Those drooping roofs should have been thatched, not slated, but otherwise the whole thing, including the grounds, was the creation of a southerner longing for home, even to Peace roses climbing the walls. Like so many English cottages, this one would have at least ten rooms tucked away behind a modest frontage, and as I walked past the door I saw why the site had been chosen. The view was charming—islands, distant mainland—an ideal spot if you could eliminate all thoughts of a million tons of rock liable to drop on you from behind. The Swiss are used to living overhung like this, but the British prefer tamer domestic settings and I had the feeling that this house had changed hands often, successive owners growing increasingly avalanche conscious. Even with the property market on its knees, it ought to be fairly easy to sell, though, with advertising beamed toward the get-away-from-the-rat-race suckers, an offer of blissful peace on a beautiful Scottish island. And if London didn't provide any takers, there was always *The New York Times.* You would have to be careful about offering the estate only in summer, when the roses were out, these making half credible a seller's chat about Arran's semitropical climate.

The roses were out for me, a first crop, great perfect heads which had the mean-minded frustrated gardener I now am at once looking for signs of black spot, which I found. There was moss in the grass, too; it was almost sixty percent moss. Half of me was suddenly wanting to take over this garden, to spend the rest of my life fighting nature for it, the other half glad I live in a penthouse with rubber plants and tubs of canna out on the terrace.

Lady Eloise's private retreat on the estate was a cedar cottage verandaed to make it look like a dark bungalow—a tropic rest house. It had been placed as far from the mock Tudor as possible, on a little promontory. There didn't seem to be any path to it; you just walked over the lawn, exposed all the way to French windows at one side of Tigh-na-Claddach. Someone wanting to contact Lady Eloise without the rest of the family knowing would either have to swim for it in waters that probably had a treacherous current or else come with wire clippers to make a hole in ten-foot-high deer fencing. That seller's ad could make quite a feature of security, too, for with a mastiff turned loose at night, the whole place was about as private as you can get these days.

The cedar cottage had no kept garden around it, just a tumble of rocks certain to receive a lot of salt spray in winter but now decorated with masses of wild sea pinks. A sort of terrace had been scraped out in front of one of the verandas and in the middle of this was a deck chair with a hand-held parasol screening the occupier. I was spotted, the parasol wobbled a greeting, but there was no movement out of the chair. The voice reached me, needing only a fraction more volume to get a real echo from the mountains.

"There is a path over to your left, Mr. Harris."

A voice had given me a picture of its owner, large-framed, big-boned, a wife formidable enough to keep even a British Resident from sleeping with native girls. The woman in the narrow deck chair didn't cover all the canvas: an undernourished Dresden shepherdess whose pink-and-white china complexion was being as carefully protected from the Scottish sun as it had been from all other suns. She looked up at me, blue eyes, head tilted back, only her neck showing age wrinkling, her face of a completely different vintage, but I couldn't believe this had been done by a surgeon; it came from a lifetime of massage discipline. She had used makeup but this was applied without any of that desperation you see so often with the old. She smiled. It seemed improbable that her teeth were her own, but if they weren't the set was a work of art.

"*So* good of you to come, Mr. Harris."

She signaled to a steel-and-canvas chair.

"Forgive me not getting up, but these days when I'm down I stay there for a long time. My old bones creak and my hands . . ."

She held out one for me to see, pale in sunlight beyond her private shade, age spots creamed away but the fingers swollen and twisted.

"Sickening, isn't it? So ugly. I mind most that it's in my hands. Feet wouldn't be so bad. I've been a painter all my life. I suppose I could learn to hold brushes in my mouth, but I haven't tried yet."

A bid for sympathy was there, but it was only a part of a larger act, a tableau staged for my benefit. It must hurt her to go on holding up that parasol, but this was an essential prop; by merely using something so basically unnecessary in the British climate, she was putting herself out of this environment, alien to it. This was round one in establishing lines of communication with me; others soon followed.

"You take after your mother's side of the family, I think. She was very dark. A handsome woman."

From Dresden china that was a deft insult. She hadn't liked my mother. Not many women did.

"I shall call you Paul. You don't mind?"

"Of course not."

"And you must call me Eloise. When you read my letter you *did* think I was a little mad?"

I was polite. "No."

She suddenly seemed diffident about what she had to say next, shy almost, not looking at me for practically the first time since I had come over the lawn and up her path.

"You see, Paul, I felt I had a special claim on you. Through your father."

There was a long pause. It was still in the sunlight, not even the sea making much noise. A car groaned on a gradient somewhere.

"I was in love with him."

My sense of shock was very slight, but it was there for all that. Fresh details about a parent's private life force you to reopen a file that has been closed and stored away for occasional reference only. Somehow I wasn't able to see my father, basically a roughish man, bedding a Dresden shepherdess. Chinese whores were more his extramarital line.

"We weren't lovers. I was faithful to John. Which was probably very silly of me. But we believed in duty in those days. It barred us from so much."

I may have been expected to probe gently, but Eloise wasn't held up for long when I didn't.

"I've been dutiful in many areas. None of them have brought me any rewards. I wish now I had followed my impulses more."

The lines of communication between us suddenly had grappling hooks at the end of them. I was about to be boarded and subjected to emotional piracy. Intimacies from the old are hard to take; there is something faintly indecent about people over seventy not having been able to reach at least a partial serenity. And for a woman of her generation and background, Lady Eloise was being appallingly un-British, implying without too much delicacy that she wished she had gone to bed with my father. Probably a suitable occasion would have been the night of the fireworks at the coronation of the rajah, with Sir John drunk and incapable. The gamelan orchestras would have been playing until the early hours and, for miles around, the Tetuan jungle offering the red flarings of feast fires. Father, looking a bit like the late Clark Gable, would suddenly throw away his cheroot and clutch Eloise to his chest. That was the moment of her big decision. She could say yes and share his passion under a mosquito net on which the *chicha* lizards dropped from the ceiling from time to time, or no and stick to duty. I might have offered the comfort that father as a lover taken could have proved considerably less memorable than as a lover denied, but kept my mouth shut.

I could see I was proving a real disappointment. She had been expecting at least a partial repeat of Papa, a robust extrovert against whose noisy maleness she would be, for all her voice, a small white dove fluttering. Instead was this unresponsive man who looked like his mother.

"Coffee, Paul?" That was abrupt, almost harsh.

It turned out she wanted some and I would have to make it from a jar of Nescafé set out in the kitchenette, my absence providing her with a lull in which she could reassess strategy. The living room was large and full of the kind of trophies from a former life that people used to bring home in the days when steamer freight charges were still reasonable—Korean chests, carved Chinese deadwood, a Tientsin carpet, much porcelain—but for an amateur painter she was extremely modest about her own work; none of this hung. In fact, the walls were completely bare of the Chinese paintings on silk and possibly Japanese prints I would have expected, just a Malay curved-bladed kris hanging on tasseled cords and one small picture on the opposite wall over a natural stone fireplace, this gilt-framed. I detoured to have a look. It seemed to be a copied Renoir, not a reproduction, rather well done, though the shadowy light didn't allow me much of a view.

In the kitchenette a tray was ready with cups and biscuits, the powdered coffee waiting, as possibly useful props in a planned campaign. All I had to do was light the bottled-gas stove. As I came out onto the veranda Eloise called out:

"There's a small folding table. Will you bring it, please?"

The mountains should have echoed the sound of that. I managed both the tray and the table and Eloise was charming about the service rendered, requesting the table pushed close so that she could reach out for refreshment with one hand. Like so many delicate, tiny-boned women, she had been able to eat what she liked all her life, and she now had three chocolate biscuits in swift succession to give her strength for what lay ahead. All through this the parasol continued to be held up in aching fingers, and though ten minutes of cloud over sun ought to have allowed her to lower it, she didn't.

If I hadn't inherited a family business, I would have made a very good waiter. I tidied up, the tray back in the kitchenette, the table up on the veranda again. I brought down her Turkish cigarettes and struck the match. When the smoke started to drift my way I was glad for once that I had given up the vice. Eloise had started on it when she was still a deb. It had been very naughty then, even though lung cancer was still diagnosed as galloping consumption. She had been quite a naughty girl, really, going to Paris at the end of her second season after coming out, this instead of marrying a duke's nephew. The duke's nephew had followed her to France, but she had been taken on at the studio of a quite well-known portrait painter, and conventional marriage was not for her, at least not then.

Eloise laughed at herself, but not very seriously.

"I was going to be an artist. My parents were furious. But they couldn't stop me. I had a little money of my own."

It wouldn't be kind to ask why she had given up art for a Colonial Service husband. Possibly it was a partial repeat of that Maugham case history about the young pianist who finds his talent *manqué* and shoots himself. Only Dresden shepherdesses of the twenties didn't shoot themselves; if it was too late to try another London season, they joined the fishing fleet to Ceylon. And if Ceylon was overcrowded with other girls angling for husbands, you moved on to Malaya, where there was usually a big selection waiting of Mr. Rights. Soon you would be able to send home that letter saying that you had found John Martin-Macintosh in the luncheon room at the Ipoh Club. It was then only a question of whether to make the long voyage for a wedding in Surrey or to fix things up quickly, always wisest, with a ceremony in Singapore's Anglican cathedral. I am personally a direct product of a slight variation on this theme. My mother was on a world tour, chaperoned by her brother, when she met my father in Shanghai.

I had failed to bring out an ashtray and Eloise didn't know what to do with her cigarette, so I took the stub and shoved it into a clump of pinks. She moved the parasol grip from one hand to the other.

"Paul, did you notice that picture in my sitting room?"

"Yes."

"You recognized the painter?"

"Copy of a Renoir?"

The canvas chair creaked.

"It is *not* a copy."

My curiosity about this woman was now satisfied to the point of satiation. It wasn't at all easy to sound even interested, let alone excited.

"Can you be certain of that?"

Eloise was staring out at me from her private shade. I could see in well enough to note that anger slightly protruded her eyes.

"I was in Paris for *two* years. Studying *art.*"

Apparently this equipped her with all those specialist skills needed to detect a forgery.

"There are a lot of Renoirs about these days that Renoir never painted."

"He painted *that* one! I can *prove* it. At today's prices it could be worth a quarter of a million pounds!"

This was certainly quite a thought, and if by any chance the painting in there was an original, I could see why Eloise had put up all that deer fencing and kept a mastiff, not safe even with these security precautions. However, I was pretty sure she was safe enough and was about to say how much I had enjoyed our meeting but had now to get back to my hotel, when she lashed words across my escape plans.

"I asked you here because I want you to take that picture to London. *And* sell it for me."

THREE

I have learned enough about the art world from the Sunday papers to know that the mere rumor that you have an original top Impressionist to dispose of will surely bring an expert from Sotheby's, or Christies, or Harwell-Speed's to your doorstep fast even if you do live on Arran. There is absolutely no need for a middleman anywhere in the deal, or a porter to carry the parcel from seller to market. I sat there thinking that though she certainly didn't look it, or sound it, Lady Martin-Macintosh was nonetheless in her dotage. I asked a gentle question.

"Is your picture signed by Renoir?"

"No."

"Didn't he usually sign his work?"

"Yes. But the painting I have is a fragment of another he painted immediately afterward."

"I don't understand."

"It's quite simple. You could say that Renoir's most famous work is 'Dancing at the Moulin de la Galette.' It's in the Louvre. And it's enormous. My picture is almost identical to the lower-right-hand corner of 'La Galette.' Almost identical, but not exactly. He was persuaded by other artist friends to paint the bigger canvas after they had seen my picture, using mine to work from. His models for 'La Galette' were mostly those other artists, who posed for all the people dancing beyond the table. Have you seen the painting?"

"Yes."

"Then you'll understand what I mean."

"What you're saying is that your picture was a tryout for 'La Galette'?"

"In a way. Though it is perfect in itself. And it is going to create a great deal of interest after being hidden for all these years."

"Where was it hidden?"

"In my husband's father's house at Rhu on the Clyde."

"Where did he get it?"

"He bought it in Paris in 1882 as a young man, paying practically nothing for it. That was before Renoir became established internationally by the dealer Paul Durand-Ruel. He was then unknown. John's father bought a lot of other pictures at the same time. They were all hung in the Rhu house and all, except the Renoir, were quite worthless."

"You're certain those others were worthless?"

"Oh, yes. They were valued from London. We got about two hundred pounds for twenty-five pictures."

"What did the valuer think of the Renoir?"

"He didn't see it."

I took time for a long, deep breath, then said:

"Which means you had identified the Renoir?"

She nodded. The parasol wobbled slightly.

"Of course. The first time I saw it. When John took me to meet his father."

"You didn't say anything about this to the family?"

"I did not. John's father wouldn't have known a Renoir from a piece of wallpaper."

"Then why did he buy pictures?"

"He had built a new house at Rhu. He wanted covering for his walls. None of his neighbors had *French* paintings."

Eloise laughed. Her businesslike replies to my questions were becoming slightly unnerving.

"Did you tell your husband about the Renoir?"

"No." That was very crisp. "John wasn't his father's heir. He had an elder brother, a bachelor, who inherited. Michael lived in the house until he died, one year before John's death."

I had to applaud cunning. You know, or at least suspect, that there is an article belonging to your husband's family which just may, in the natural course of things, become the property of your husband and make you rich, so you don't chat about it. The thought of that Renoir in Rhu must have weighed rather heavily on Lady Eloise during the years out East, all kinds of little niggles like whether or not conditions in the house were causing it to deteriorate. She must also have burned quite a bit of private joss against the possibility of her brother-in-law's marrying late in life and producing an heir.

My questions became cautious, but I needn't have bothered; Eloise was quite ready to answer them. I lit another Russian cigarette for her and she sat back in the chair, looking at me all the time, occasionally shifting the weight of that parasol, but never letting it droop.

John's father had been the chairman of MacArthur's Steamship Company, once very well known, with at least thirty cargo-passenger liners with which they had made quite a killing in the immigrant trade, as useful in its time as slavery had been to the clippers. After the First World War the firm had gone into a sharp decline, becoming bankrupt in the Depression. As so often happens with company chairmen, the elder Martin-Macintosh had been able to save a reasonable personal fortune from the wreckage, but his son Michael had acquired the spending habit early and never learned to work. When John came to inherit only a year before his own death, there hadn't been much more than the Rhu house and its contents. Eloise didn't say so, but it was quite plain that if Michael had ever found out about that Renoir it would have been at a London salesroom the next day and he would have been off on another of the round-the-world cruises which were his weakness, together with the bottle.

The idea that a woman can't keep a secret has always seemed remarkably silly to me. Eloise had tucked this one away for all those years in the Orient, much of the time living with assorted distressing nightmares about how that painting could slip away from her. One of them might well be that John died before his elder brother, leaving his widow with scant claim to anything from Michael's estate.

"I can see what you're thinking," Eloise said, giving me the uneasy feeling that she probably could. "I'm an amateur painter, but that doesn't mean I would know a real Renoir from a good copy. Well, I *would.* But remember this: the picture in my sitting room was painted, and bought by my father-in-law, years before Renoir was worth anyone's time to copy."

I took her point. It was a good one, likely to arouse a London dealer's interest at once. A young Scottish businessman had gone to Paris in 1882 and bought a batch of pictures to hang in his new house, and with the junk came the Renoir.

"Paul, let the picture talk to you. Go in and have another look at it. In the long drawer in my desk you'll find a reproduction of the Louvre 'La Galette.' "

The suggestion was sensible, and I also wanted to be alone for a few minutes. I went in and switched on the painting's private light, looking at it first from a distance, then close up. It was charming, though perhaps a bit crowded, six people packed in about a café table with an enchantingly pretty girl in a summer dress full face toward her boyfriend, who had his back turned. An older woman, bending forward over the table, had an arm about the girl's shoulders, with another even older woman seated just beyond her. Two young men and the profile of a second girl at an adjoining table made up the group. I stared at them all for quite some time, beginning to get the strange feeling that Renoir *was* talking to me, via a house on the Clyde where a portion of him had been in hiding for more than ninety years.

The photograph of the Louvre's "La Galette" rated the whole of the drawer, lying flat, and I stood with it in my hand. The fragment was similar without in any way being a detail from the big canvas. In "La Galette" the seated older woman is turned away, only the back of her head and one ear visible. Both the young men in the Louvre painting wear hats, though hatless in Eloise's version, but the thing that impressed me most was the way that the colored photograph seemed to manage only a faint reflection of that light in the faces of the women that was so marked in the painting on the wall, as though they were illuminated by some inner joy vitalizing a moment of living. No painter has ever loved his women more than Renoir, and under his hands even the old are young, but the reproduction hardly began to make this apparent.

I was more than slightly shaken. The picture's owner was waiting for a verdict I wasn't qualified to give. I went slowly down the steps. Eloise watched me settle again in the chair, but said nothing. I sensed a kind of triumph coming from her, as though she had seen in my face what she wanted to see and that was enough. A tanker was coming up the estuary, one of the big ones, bound for the specially constructed docks on Loch Long. With its towering stern superstructure, it looked like a galleon of the new age bringing dubious treasure.

"Why are you selling now?" I asked.

"I have to. It's my inheritance. And my last chance. If I stay here I'll die soon. Every winter I get worse. My body's curling up. In the sun that would stop. The arthritis mayn't be cured, but it won't get worse."

"Where in the sun?"

"Ootacamund."

That suggested India, but I had no idea where on the subcontinent. She told me. It was the hill station for Madras. In the days of the British raj, the local governor and his court had moved up for the season, bringing considerable pomp and ceremony. Some of this was still maintained by the Indian proconsul under Mrs. Nehru, who also shifted his administration up into the mountains for the very hot season, and at the end of this holiday a retreat was beaten just as it had been in the old days, the new flag lowered at sunset, with a brass band playing. There was also still an Ootacamund Hunt and a Hunt Ball, this supported by the surviving British, a small colony of diehards who had refused to leave India. Servants were cheap, or at least cheaper than anywhere else, and Eloise's best friend, Mabel, had moved there from Malaysia via two years in Brighton, which had been enough to make her decide that was all she wanted of England. You still woke in the morning to your chota hazri, brought on a tray by a turbaned domestic, and your day was totally free of housework. You gardened gently early in the morning, with a Tamil to do the serious digging, and in the afternoons and evenings played bridge. The sunset flamed for your first drink of the day. But the best thing about "Snooty Ooty" was that no one, except old Far Eastern hands, had ever heard of it, and there was no new colony of beatniks or escapers from the British winter, not even a hint of the too rich to shove up living costs for the retired.

Mabel's letters kept urging Eloise to come out and share her house. Things weren't quite like the old days, of course—she now had only three indoor servants and two outside, plus a man to drive the Morris Minor—but compared to "home" it was still a paradise in which the sun toasted old bones. Further, the Indians were kind to these vestigial hangovers from the raj, rather pleased to have them as historical relics who helped keep up many of the old imperial traditions for which the natives retained a sneaking affection still. Ooty was the antithesis of most of the new pushing post-colonial societies, a gentle backwater in which the seasons came and went with almost imperceptible signs of change. Mabel said that the view from her main veranda was over rolling hills that could have been the

English South Downs a hundred years before the developers reached them. All her letters were on the theme of come, come; two survivors from another world to live together without stress, sharing memories of what could never be again while someone else did the cooking. In Ootacamund your parasol was not a defiant gesture against place and change, you really needed to use one, especially when watching tennis. Some of the younger residents, still only in their sixties, managed to go on playing tennis. There was the Ooty Club, where the Hunt Ball was held and where there was bridge and on gala nights even dancing.

"Have you ever lived in India?"

Eloise shook her head. "John and I once had a holiday in Darjeeling. I know it won't be the same as Malaya or Borneo, but near enough. Have you a cook these days in Singapore?"

"No."

"There, you *see?* It's quite impossible. I hear it's nothing but skyscrapers and horrible new hotels."

She looked suddenly at the oil tanker, moving slowly, still in view.

"I don't want this place any longer. I don't *want* it!"

It ought to be possible to live quite well in Ooty on a quarter of a million, or even considerably less. Eloise might even become queen of the place, holding court on Tuesdays.

"And what about Tigh-na-Claddach?"

"Anne can have it." She added, as if I might as well be given the whole picture, "She's not really my child. John and I had no children. We adopted Anne when she was six weeks old. The daughter of a district officer who died. His wife was a fast woman who wanted to be free to live her own life. So we took Anne."

She didn't add that this was something she had never regretted, the usual politeness.

"Why do you want *me* to take the picture to London?"

"Because I know I can trust your father's son."

A tribute to my parent left me unmoved.

"Why not just ring up Christies and ask them to send their expert?"

"I've already done it. Not Christies, Harwell-Speed. Only a few months ago."

I was most interested. "What was his verdict?"

Eloise didn't answer at once. She was now staring toward the main house at Tigh-na-Claddach. When she did speak, it was with deep bitterness.

"We were *charged* for his expenses. And he was a fool! He said my Renoir is a good copy. Made about 1910. He just wouldn't listen when I told him that couldn't be, that it isn't a copy of anything!"

So Renoir hadn't really been talking to me up there in the sitting room. The expert from Harwell-Speed would have come here desperately hoping that he was going to find a mislaid Renoir, the kind of happening which simply makes any top-class auction house's month, and that man could have been literally trembling when he stepped on Eloise's veranda for the first time. I could see him walking toward a stone fireplace, hope still there, flaring even, then the big letdown from closer inspection, a deep sadness its by-product. By 1910 Renoir was well worth faking, fetching big prices for the time. Eloise would not have had her first look at the painting until well into the twenties, after she had married John. She had simply accepted her father-in-law's word that he had bought the picture more than forty years earlier and he had then been a very old man, his memory probably totally unreliable.

"You could always get a second opinion."

Eloise glared. "I don't need a second opinion. That picture will be recognized as a Renoir by any competent art expert."

"A man from Harwell-Speed is likely to be as competent as you'll find."

"Well, this one wasn't! So you're like the others, Paul? Ready to believe one so-called expert?"

"By the others you mean your daughter and her husband?"

"Yes. They think I'm an old fool. Anne listens to Angus. God knows why. A lot of good he's ever done her in anything. The man's a parasite and always has been. Do you know this: he lives off me! I bought this place and provided them with that house over there. I also bought Angus the garage he goes to all week on the mainland. It has cost me almost every penny I have to set those two up, to give them a home and provide Angus with another business for him to ruin. I didn't want to come to Scotland after John died; I did it to please Anne and that creature she married. You'd think they were doing *me* a kindness, allowing me to exist at the edge of their lives like this. Of course, it was very silly of me to expect gratitude from an adopted daughter. She's not the sort to consider the kind of life she would have had if John and I hadn't taken her in. Her own mother wouldn't have done much for her, I can tell you that!"

The parasol was now shaking. Eloise's self-dedication was total, as incurable as her arthritis. I was being sucked into a domestic situation about which I could do nothing even if I wanted to, caught in a bog while out on a casual stroll, already up to my knees and sinking fast.

"Help me into the house!"

That was a command. Getting her out of the deck chair wasn't easy; in the process I had to take the parasol and close it, leaving her exposed to the sun, her face marred by anger, lines from her throat suddenly invading it. From the way she dragged in her breath on the steps up to the veranda it seemed likely she had a heart condition, but it could have been just fury raising blood pressure.

There was a special chair for Eloise by a fireplace in which logs were set but unlit. The room was chill after outside and I switched on an electric heater, directing the beam toward her. She was staring at me again.

"Why shouldn't I do what I want? You think I should just stay here? Because I'm old? When you're old your life is over. You're supposed to sit waiting patiently. Well, I'm not going to! I'm going to Ootacamund!"

"All right!"

Anger was beamed straight at me. I might have been a son who had failed her.

"It's *not* all right! I can't go unless I sell the Renoir. I won't live with Mabel if I'm poor. I'm not a charity case. I must get the money for that picture."

"I can't help you do it."

"You mean you won't try?"

"It's no use my trying. It's a thousand to one against another London auction house disagreeing with the Harwell-Speed man. But if you must have a second opinion, or a third, that will be easy enough."

"You mean have them here? Anne wouldn't let anyone else come."

"How can she stop you? This is your property."

"She could—"

Eloise broke off. She stared for a moment at the red patch the heater put on a rug, then her head dropped forward, her shoulders began to shake. The noise she made was a kind of sniveling, horrible to listen to, a whining of feeble old age. Those clawed hands were clamped down onto the chair's arm, swollen fingers digging into upholstery.

"Oh, Paul . . . you were my hope. . . ."

I felt sick. Then, as suddenly as it had started, the scene ended, but the star actress wasn't sitting exhausted behind a dropped curtain. Her head jerked up, she stared toward the painting, her voice once again for the back of the upper gallery.

"That *is* a Renoir!"

From the door to the veranda a voice said:

"Oh, Mother! You're not at *that* again!"

I walked with Anne across the kind of west Highland lawn I had heard a Scottish gardening authority say could be cured of moss sickness only by a pet reindeer. Lady Eloise hadn't ordered us out of the bungalow; she just sat like an effigy, refusing to speak, while the temperature, in spite of two bars on the heater, plummeted.

Anne was in her late twenties, possibly early thirties, tall, fair, leggy, just missing good looks, but with a kind of gangling sexuality she knew how to exploit. It may have been the elasticity underfoot, but she moved with a curious lope, as though adjusting a hill walker's stride to my restricted pace, made slightly awkward herself in the process. She had big hands, far from tiny feet, and very blue eyes, which I saw through a shine of hair, since she did not really turn her head when she spoke.

"Where's your car, Mr. Harris?"

"Your mother told me on the phone where to hide it."

"Oh, God! I'm responsible for this."

"Why?"

"I told her last night, when I took over her milk drink, that Angus had seen you. I should have known better, but—well, it's not easy to find anything to talk about with Mother. You were from the East, and Angus knew who you were, and you were staying at the whorehouse."

"Is that what it's called? There's only the word 'hotel' left on the sign."

She laughed. "It hasn't ever been exactly automobile-club-recommended for family parties. The wife of the man who runs it is a nympho. I thought it was shut, except for the bar."

"I needed a bed and a Major Henderson-Pratt fixed it up with George."

"What was the price of that? A bottle of whisky for Hendy?"

"Just about. You know him well?"

"Angus plays golf with him sometimes. I once made up a foursome with his wife. I didn't really want a repeat. She's one of those women who give you another installment on her health every time you reach a green and sometimes on the fairways, too. I can't match it. There's never been much wrong with my health."

We had reached the rose beds.

"You'll come in and have a drink? I expect you need it."

"Yes," I said.

"Poor Ma. It's so sad, really. But I feel awful that you were involved. All my fault."

"Not your fault at all. Your mother wrote me. I came."

Anne stopped by a successful bush of red Ena Harkness. "She *what?*"

"The letter was forwarded from a business I used to have. Your mother had read about my being in Scotland. She knew my father."

Anne stood there sucking in a long, deep breath, then said, "I see. The old are cunning. Never a word to me, of course. So all I did last night was announce that you had arrived? You'd have come even if Mother hadn't phoned?"

"That was my idea."

"Do you go around asking for trouble, Mr. Harris?"

"It's a tendency I ought to curb."

Our feet crunched on gravel. A green Mini was parked near the front door.

"Are you psychic in matters concerning your mother?"

She gave me that look through her hair.

"You mean my quick return from Brodick? In a way I suppose I am. But when I got to town and saw Mother's list it struck me pretty forcibly that she'd asked for a lot of things I knew she didn't need. And which would involve me in going into every shop in the place. You could say that was when I had my flash of intuition. But how did you time your arrival so beautifully?"

"I was hiding in some bushes when you passed on the way out. What have you done with that dog?"

"He's inside. I never take him to the bungalow. Mother hates him. Poor Rufus, he's really a silly old poppet."

Practically a quarter of a ton of silly old poppet was waiting for us in the inner hall, and with a series of barks which sounded as though thunder had got inside the house. However, I was properly introduced and a beautifully trained docility, demonstrated by Rufus's being made to give me a paw which I couldn't feel, sealed our relationship for all time. Mastiffs tend to drool a bit and this one was doing it. I didn't like the red veining in his eyes.

The sitting room was furnished totally without trophies from the East and rather cheaply, but pleasantly chintzy, and with long windows commanding a view of the bungalow across grass. There was a fireplace in which even in summer logs smoldered. The place smelled faintly of smoke from resinous wood and dog.

"Whisky?"

"Please."

I guessed right, she was a whisky drinker, too, the kind of girl who sat low in a deep chair when she had her glass, with long, trousered legs thrust out. Even when I had her full face one eye was screened with blond hair. Anne wouldn't look smart in an evening dress, but wearing one, would still contrive to make chic women seem ordinary. With that great dog lolling at her feet, she could have been the huntress Diana resting; all that was needed was her bow dropped on the Persian rug. She didn't mention her husband, so I assumed he was over on the mainland losing money in the business that had been bought for him.

"Is there any hope the picture *is* a Renoir?"

She shook her head. "I wish there was. The whole thing has become a dreadful obsession. You've no idea what it's like to live with."

I could guess.

"Does your mother do for herself over there?"

Anne laughed. "My mother has never done for herself. I take over meals. Not breakfast, but everything else. She sometimes makes her own morning coffee. When she isn't eating she broods and plays patience."

"With all these ex-Far Eastern hands about, hasn't she any friends on the island?"

"They're not the right kind of ex-Far Eastern hands. Once you've lived in a residency you never forget it."

"Why not just let her go to Otacamund?"

"It's a crazy dream. She and Mabel would start fighting after the first week. At that age you can't just go lunging into something new. My mother doesn't love me all that dearly and she really hates Angus, but we're family. So what do you do? You go on, that's all."

Anne sipped whisky, then said, "Mother told you I'm not her flesh and blood?"

"Yes."

"Give her an hour and she can really put someone in the picture. The right someone, that is. How do you qualify?"

I told her, without mentioning smoldering passion on Tetuan. She listened, most of the time with her glass lifted, looking at me over the rim. Rufus was now asleep, seemingly having a dream in which he was chasing a wildcat up one of the high corries behind the house. Anne asked a few questions, then it was my turn.

"How long have you known about the Renoir?"

"You mean how long have I known that Mother thinks it's worth a quarter of a million? Only a few months. I knew she valued the thing, of course. It was in their house down south and she was always fussy about where she put it—not too much sunlight, enough heat, and so on. I thought she was potty, but then she paints herself, or used to. What I know about art is a vast nothing and I just wasn't interested. Though I did notice that when we got this place and she moved her stuff up, the picture had a special crate. Practically air-conditioned. Like the way they sent the 'Mona Lisa' to Japan. I believe that Ma would have gone on keeping me in the dark if she could have done, but once she'd decided to have it valued that was impossible.

The man who came might want to make tests and things, and set up cameras. Not that he did much in that line when he arrived. All he needed was half an hour in the bungalow before coming over with the bad news. I had Mother here and kept Angus out of the way. If they're in a room together they start spitting at once, that is if she acknowledges the fact that he's there. It would be quite funny if it wasn't so awful. You're a good interrogator, Mr. Harris. You're making me run on; I don't usually."

"Call me Paul. What did the man from Harwell-Speed actually say?"

"Not a great deal. He was embarrassed. Something about how it was quite a good bid to paint in the manner of Renoir and might have some value as a curiosity. You can imagine how Ma took off. Rufus was in the study, but he thought there was a riot and started barking. Quite an afternoon. I got our doctor and he administered a sedative. Our visitor from London looked as though he needed one, too. He cleared off by the evening boat. We got the bill later. Did you hear that?"

"Yes. What did you think of the expert?"

"Oh, Lord, I'm not awfully good about people. He was frightfully London, you know. From the hub and wanting back there quickly. Don't think he'd ever been in Scotland before and he wasn't likely to repeat the experience in a hurry. When he traveled it would be to Perugia looking for old ivories or something."

"You're very good indeed about people. You thought he knew his business?"

"Oh, absolutely. He gave me the feeling that he was completely used to deciding on the spot whether something was worth half a million or only about fifty pence. And Harwell-Speed are madly big-time, aren't they?"

"Yes."

"They were Ma's choice. That's what made her so furious. She had been totally knowledgeable about who to go to and all that. Angus and I weren't any use. Angus's idea of art is collecting Toby jugs, and I won't let him."

"You hadn't ever believed that it could be a Renoir?"

She thought about that.

"Not really."

"So you weren't disappointed?"

"How could I be, since I hadn't believed for a moment we'd get real money for the thing? When my uncle's place on the Clyde was sold up, the other pictures in it weren't worth anything. I suppose Ma told you about that?"

"Yes."

"She's fairly covered things. You were also told that this is a grace-and-favor house and that we're entirely dependent on her?"

"Yes."

"If I were a bit more sensitive I'd have the feeling of being left quite naked. But it isn't true. She did put money in Angus's business, but she gets a return on it. Better than she would from shares. Angus is doing very well, really."

I didn't believe her and she knew it, which forced her to go on with a stated case.

"When Father died, Ma couldn't stay on her own. The house down south was far too big, for one thing. Also, Father's annuities stopped. But she got a good price when she sold up, enough to buy this and have some left over to put in Angus's garage. She came to us because she had to be looked after, moaning a bit about having to live in Scotland. Especially on an island."

"You wanted to live on Arran?"

"Well, yes. I've always liked the country. And in spite of that ferry in winter, this is really quite handy for Angus. He commutes by sea instead of by car. And mostly he's only back at the weekends. There's a little flat over the garage office. Why am I telling you all this?"

In a moment she answered that herself.

52

"It's a relief to talk to someone, I suppose." She smiled. "And with you Ma has laid the foundations so well. We don't really have any close friends here. The people with money on the island are always back from Greek holidays we can't afford and the poor are as dull as hell, wondering which is going to finsh them off first, heart attacks or inflation. Half the people who've settled here wish they'd gone to the Canaries instead. Or New Zealand. Only New Zealand isn't taking the British poor anymore. Can you blame them? We kicked them in the teeth over the Common Market and now they don't want us. Are you rich enough to live anywhere?"

"I survive."

"These days that means you're stinking. Lucky man. Has your wife got sixteen servants?"

"I haven't got a wife."

"Divorced?"

"Widower."

"Oh. Recent?"

"Long ago."

"So why not do something about it?"

"My patterns are too hectic to allow for domesticity."

Anne laughed. "The perfect excuse for the sweet life. Lovely Chinese piece three nights a week. I was brought up in the East; I know all about it."

She didn't know all that much about contemporary Southeast Asia, her Orient half a dream from childhood never really updated by her stay there as an adult, and central to it was a Chinese amah, her surrogate mother, whose job had been, in the main, to keep the child out of Eloise's way. I knew exactly what Anne had felt about that amah because I'd had one, too, whose role was to keep my mother's afternoons free for bridge and her evenings clear for dinner parties. Mornings didn't come into it because Mother never got up in the mornings. It was a great life for parents; you had to go to the bother of producing the young yourselves, of course—unless you were Eloise—but after that you never changed a diaper. The houses were so big, also, that you really weren't ever forced to be made aware of the fact that the little beasts were about the place. Every now and then you felt in the mood to see them and did, my father pretty punctilious about this on the whole, teaching me how to sail a boat and shoot. Apparently John Martin-Macintosh had done his duty here, taking his adopted daughter for walks through the botanic gardens and sometimes to the pictures. In Tetuan going to the pictures stopped because the one cinema stank and was invariably crowded with local rowdies contriving to make totally obscene Hollywood's then relatively soft-footed approaches to sex.

"Oh, Paul, I've never told anyone this, but when I'm in Glasgow on my own there's a Chinese restaurant I always go to. I have to. It's a kind of compulsion. And as soon as I hear Cantonese I want to weep all over the bowls of food a Malay sow wouldn't eat."

"You'd like to go back?"

"God, don't talk about it!"

"When you married Angus you thought you'd be living out there?"

"Yes. We only had a year. Not quite. Then he was sent home. We had a ridiculous little house in K.L., rented from a Chinese landlord. It didn't even have a garden, just a sort of courtyard with one of those sensitive trees in it. You rub the bark low down and the whole thing shakes. You know them?"

"Sure. You met Angus out there?"

She nodded. "I was between jobs as a secretary in London. I flew out for a month. Angus was over in Tetuan for his company. After that I took a job in K.L. for a while and then we got married."

"You didn't want to go back to London?"

"No. I was telling you about that courtyard. It didn't get any real sun. I couldn't grow much, which was maddening. . . ."

She broke off, had a sip of whisky, put the glass down, then said, "But I don't have to tell you things, do I? You know. It's a curious feeling. Where do you live now?"

"Singapore, in a flat on a roof. Over a stinking river."

"Why?"

"I built the place. I thought I'd like it."

"But you don't?"

"No."

"Where would you like to live?"

"In Trengganu. By one of those twenty-mile beaches. Facing the China Sea."

"I was born just south of there. In Kuantan. Would it be a wooden house back in the palms?"

"I'd choose a site with casuarinas. I like them better. A million mosquitoes and no air conditioning."

She was staring at me. "Why don't you?"

"Lonely on my own."

"No man has to be lonely on his own. As you know damn well."

She got up. "Another drink?"

"No, thanks. I must be going."

She didn't try to stop me. "I'll drive you to where you hid your car. You're not coming, Rufus."

In the Mini she was very close, large hands on the wheel competent, but her gear change wasn't smooth.

"Needs a new clutch. Everything in this place is dropping to pieces. It seemed a snip when we got it, at today's prices, but half the drains are blocked. And the paintwork is down to the wood."

"The garden is beautiful. You do it all yourself?"

"Yes. Compensation for frustrated maternal instincts or something. We can't have kids. It's Angus. We found that out. But I've never fancied being impregnated from a test tube. You'll have to get out and open the gate."

I did that and got back in again. Our shoulders were in contact. At the side road she braked.

"Don't worry about Mother. She'll be all right. Or as right as she's going to be. And it's not your fault. How long are you staying in that ghastly place?"

"Depends on the weather. When you get a spell like this in Scotland it makes sense to enjoy it. Have dinner with me tonight in Brodick?"

"I can't."

"Tomorrow?"

"No, I'm afraid not. But . . ."

"Yes?"

"You could give me a ring. We could go for a walk, perhaps. Up the glen behind here."

I would walk up that valley between those black mountains with Anne if there was no reasonable alternative.

"Fine," I said, and got out.

She leaned over to look at me through the open window. "I like you, Paul Harris."

"In that case it's mutual."

She smiled. "Pity I'm not an Aishah."

She scraped the Mini into second, then turned the car in one sweep on the narrow road, not waving to me as she went.

FOUR

I sat in the Avenger, parked on the Brodick esplanade, leafing over the pages of *The Scottish Field,* looking for an ad I remembered from having glanced at the magazine in a hotel lounge a few days back. Harwell-Speed had taken a whole page exhorting those who lived in big old houses with large attics to have a look through these for family treasures which might have lain there undisturbed for a century or two. There were six pictures of assorted objects, from silver services to Dutch flower paintings, which had recently fetched fat prices at their London auction rooms, all of these from north of the border. At the bottom was the name of the firm's Scottish representative, the Honorable Jeffrey Fanning-Mackie, Arshignaig House, by Crinan, Argyll. There was a phone number and I went to a call box not twenty yards away, dialing and getting through at once.

"Fanning-Mackie here."

I pressed the button and explained my business, which was a shade complex, but the Honorable Jeffrey seemed to have a sharp mind.

"You want the name of a chap from our firm who valued a painting on Arran a few months ago? Why?"

It was a good question.

"Stupidly, when I was with these people I didn't ask your expert's name. And I don't want to raise the matter with them again. Actually, they're pretty upset about it still. They were so sure they had something good."

"Oh, Lord! One of those things. Happens all the time. The number of Victorian teapots I've had shoved at me as Georgian straight from Great-Great-Great-Uncle Harry. And they damn well won't believe you when you tell 'em the truth. Think you're a nit. Impressionist, you say? Renoir? That doesn't sound too likely. Our man from London . . . now who the hell would that be? If I sound a bit vague it's because I've been at the company's branch in New York for two years. Only just shoved up to my native heath. Our rivals were digging in up here and we thought we'd better, too. I was the only half-Scotsman on the firm's books so I got the job. Actually, it's damn interesting. Up here hasn't been fine-tooth-combed like down south. I got me an unknown Raeburn. Don't really know much about pictures myself, but I smelled this was the real thing and whipped it off to London. It was. Laurel wreath for the new boy in Scotia. I say, who *are* you? I don't know any Harrises."

"I'm a Singapore businessman."

"Really? Know anything about ceramics?"

"A bit."

"Splendid. You couldn't get hold of any Ming, could you? Japanese buying it like mad just now. Some Chinese tycoon who doesn't know he has it?"

"They all know when they have it these days."

"Pity. You want that name. Hang on a minute; I'll have to look it up."

There was a pause, then Fanning-Mackie came back on the line.

"It would seem to be Dennis Hodson. I've never met him, actually. He came to us after I was in America. And I've got a feeling he's left us again. Look, can I ring you back? I've got to be onto London this afternoon anyway. What's your hotel number on Arran?"

"I've forgotten it. Can I ring you?"

"Yes, do. About seven. You want to talk to Hodson, is that it?"

"If it's at all possible."

"Do you know anything about Impressionist painting yourself?"

"I look at them when I get the chance."

"Not a collector?"

"I have a three-roomed flat. I don't collect anything."

"This damn contemporary living in boxes. Ridiculous! I've got a fourteen-roomed house here. It's driving my wife quite mad. She says she hadn't expected ever again to even see a slow-combustion solid-fuel cooker, let alone have to live with one. And she's having to do it, poor thing. But actually it's quite bliss after a New York apartment. We've got twelve acres. If you're ever in Crinan, come in and have a drink."

"Thanks. I may be there in a day or two. I've just found out there's a small ferry from Lochranza here over to Kintyre."

"Sure. You take it. I have to be in Inverness on Thursday, but otherwise, unless there's a sudden call somewhere, I ought to be at home. A bogus Renoir, eh?"

"So your man Hodson told them."

"I might as well tell *you*, Harris, that I don't think our man is likely to be proved wrong."

"I know that."

"Well, forgive me asking this, but what's biting you?"

"It's hard to say. But I liked the picture. They were Renoir faces. The women, I mean."

"Eh? Oh. Quality of painting, is that it? And you have a sort of hunch about it, as I did with the Raeburn?"

"I wouldn't put it as strongly as that."

"But you still want to know more? All right, I'll try to get hold of Hodson for you. A phone number or something. He'll give you the facts. The firm will know where he is if he has left us. Probably with a rival. 'Bye just now."

I went back to the car feeling something of a fool.

It was a sunny day, warm, promising to get even warmer. The thing to do was improvise a picnic, then find a beach somewhere. I bought the picnic and took the road along which I had torn down the swami posters, from Brodick to Blackwater Foot, turning south from there to a point where the road swung inland. Just before it did, there was a motorable track down to the shore and I was able to park the Avenger only a few feet from a little cove with white sand, protected by two natural rock walls and offering a view due west to the long peninsula of Kintyre. There was a lull in air traffic, only sea noise to be heard, and miles away across the sound sunlight glinted on the windshield of a car using the road past Carradale.

I lay back and dozed, pretty soon returned to Kuala Lumpur, up on that hill behind the city where there are now three new apartment blocks with sun balconies, but the site haunted by another house that once stood there, a sprawling bungalow with wide verandas to trap the breeze and usher it through cool, high rooms. This time I wasn't alone in that house. A woman came across rough, blue-bladed grass harshly disciplined into lawn, wearing gardening gloves, a trowel in one of them, coming to me.

I woke with Anne in my mind and body, that burning between two people suddenly stopped in their separate and often distant patterns by a total consciousness of one another. I don't know anything about telepathy, just that this happens, to be joy or pain or lust so acute it wipes out everything else for a time. I brought in reason for perspective, but reason let me down. I put ham inside a roll and swallowed to activate my stomach, concentrating blood there, but after two rolls and half a can of beer Anne was still signaling. If this went on it was going to mean getting an old Chinese house for conversion somewhere outside Singapore on the road to Changi. The garden would be left to her and most of the alterations. I could see her sliding into that scheme with the ease of someone who has already known the East, celebrating her return as a kind of triumph. There was a lot going for what I had to offer besides me. Angus could have custody of Rufus. He had been right to dislike me at sight.

I couldn't really believe in the noise of that transistor, though it was loud enough, bursting from the next cove over a partition of rocks. I can't forgive the Japanese for having popularized that thing and equipping it with volume loud enough to fill a concert hall, this volume always turned up full in a rape of silence. The most awful curse laid on contemporary man isn't the atomic threat, or pollution; it is boxed din wherever he goes.

I got up, only just remembering to collect my litter, backing the car to a turning place, never even seeing the perpetrators of the outrage, anger somehow swollen by what I had just been planning for my future. I drove badly on a narrow road, coming around a bend too fast too far out, scaring into open mouths a family party in an Austin Maxi. The hotel with no name except the one Anne had given it sat in a heat-absorbing vacuum made by trees, the birds sun-drugged, the stillness dedicated. At three in the afternoon all the doors were shut, even the one to the bar, the lower windows blank from no real living behind them. I got out of the car and looked up.

Aishah was standing right up against the glass in one of the windows of my bedroom. She was wearing a cardigan but suddenly, smiling, put her hands up under it to her breasts and slowly, very slowly, ran palms down her body to her thighs. Then she disappeared, presumably to wait for me on that memorable bed.

The invitation had been issued at the wrong moment for me psychologically and I didn't accept, going to an iron bench at the far side of the hayfield, lighting up one of the cigars I permit myself only at times of acute stress. It was tropic hot, the buzzing I heard coming at first only from amiable insects using a buddleia in bloom, but then came midges, a revolving, pulsing genie cloud of them. I broke up the formation with smoke, but they then attacked singly from all angles until I had to move, going along a path almost overgrown by rhododendrons, which landed me at the hotel garbage dump, heavily colonized by flies. From here was a view of the back of the building, more dead windows, the lower ones barred. The huge pile didn't look at all like a whorehouse, more an open borstal handed back to the original owners some years earlier, who had taken their compensation for extensive damage and used it to buy a villa in Majorca. A projecting annex had to be the kitchens, but there was no sign of any activity there, a solid door shut, not even a dish towel hanging on a line. There had been no hints so far of any staff besides Aishah and George helping to run this place, no morning hum of vacuum cleaners, and though my bedroom and the bathroom seemed reasonably well maintained, I had felt crunching underfoot on bits of threadbare carpeting.

The woods formed an inner enclave of what had been a much larger estate, and since the original planting there had been no thinning out, tall trunks competing for light, their lower branches atrophied. I went on into deep shadow where it was cool, moving in that afternoon phase which hits travelers everywhere, when there is really damn all to do except wait for the next meal if you have declined going to bed with the proprietor's wife. I hit another path and stayed with it to a small clearing in which there was the ruin of a little Victorian gazebo. This had once had a thatched roof, now crumbled away, exposing rotting timbers going up to a peak like the framework for an Indian tepee. Long ago the boredom of house parties had been relieved by the delicious novelty of tea out here among the midges. A dozen parasols like Eloise's had once bobbed over deck chairs and polite chatter. There must have been a view from this architectural whimsy in those days, but there wasn't now, scrub growth and brambles blotting it out.

It would have been a natural place in which to find a body,

or at least a skeleton. I found something else, a path behind the gazebo which seemed newly made, leading down by rough steps into what could have been the forest nest for some vast animal, except that its center was filled with something made by man. I stared with the eerie feeling of having been transported half a world away, this time when awake. A small hut was built mostly of sapling poles and it was mounted on these, too, a slatted floor raised a good four feet above the ground as semiprotection against snakes and scorpions. Access to the interior was by a ladder and a strip of veranda, the whole roofed with thatching taken from the gazebo. Except for that roofing, which should have been palm leaves, this was a tiny replica of a Malay hut, one of those casual little shelters which a tropic forest people live in for a season or two and then abandon, moving on to another jungle clearing to build once again.

I went up two rungs of the ladder and peered into the tiny, windowless compartment. There was just about enough room inside for one person, and a small person at that. The place was in use, a woven mat rolled up and tucked in one corner, a Woolworth mirror hanging on a nail, with a white towel on another, but the things that interested me most were two small pottery bowls set out on the slats of the veranda, both with hardened traces of food sticking to them. That food hadn't been put there for the birds; it was Aishah's offering to the spirits of a Scottish wood.

I climbed down the ladder, an intruder, standing to listen and soon hearing the soft sound of water, a small stream nearby. There was access to it, not by another path but by a tunnel through undergrowth that would have to be used on all fours. The little burn would have been dammed with rocks to make a pool where a Sino-Malay ex-dance hostess could bathe when the weather was like today's. The girl, born on Singapore island, had probably never even seen the real rain forest or one of the huts built for shelter in them, the design of this retreat having been part of some race memory direct from one line of her ancestors. It was almost impossible that she had made all this herself, George must have helped her, and there was something almost grimly pathetic in the thought of that red-faced former policeman pandering to the half-child in Aishah, creating for her a let's-pretend hideaway and then never following her here when she wanted to use it. Only a man very near to desperation could allow himself to believe that this kind of therapy had any hope of being effective.

A twig cracked. There was a faint rustling. My retreat up to the gazebo clearing and beyond it was as noisy as a buffalo's.

The smell in the front hall as I stood at the telephone table told me that the evening menu was built around fried fish Écossais. The ringing at the other end of the line was broken by a woman's cool, brisk voice.

"Jane Fanning-Mackie."

"I'm Paul Harris. Your husband is expecting my call."

"Oh, yes." There was a pause. "Jeff said you might be coming to see us?"

"Perhaps a look in on my way north."

"Do." That was even cooler. "I'll get him."

I heard the receiver put down on mahogany and then the voice, still audible, though some distance away.

"Jeff? It's the man you asked to come here. From Singapore or somewhere."

Jane Fanning-Mackie sounded as though she was the one who defended the family's privacy. Jeff was wheezing a bit when he picked up the receiver.

"Harris? Sorry to keep you. I was bringing in some logs. Spend half my life sawing the damn things, but they do make a marvelous fire. Don't go for peat myself—it stinks like wet tweed. Well, I was onto London this afternoon and Hodson *has* left us. Though that's perhaps not quite the way to put it, from the sound of things. Head office was being cagey; they wanted to know who was asking about our former employee, so I said a rich Far Eastern merchant and that made them even cagier. But from all this I did rather gather that Hodson had gone under something of a cloud, and not a small one either. Probably some breach of ethics."

"Ethics?"

"Don't sound so surprised. Auctioneers and valuers, in our area of the field at any rate, live by a stricter ethic these days than most doctors."

"Really?"

He laughed. "If you're going to be such a damn skeptic, consider that invitation to drinks canceled. However, I'll admit that we're highly moral because it pays off. You need all kinds of integrity labels tied on you before a chap with a million-pound Monet to sell trusts you to do it. Get the point?"

"I'm beginning to."

"Well, that's us, Harwell-Speed: never the smallest spot on our escutcheon for over eighty years."

"At twenty percent of million-pound Monets, you can afford to be ethical."

"There is that, of course. Hodson must have done something that at least threatened a stain on the old snow-white mantle. But they wouldn't tell me over the phone just what he had been up to."

"You'll get it out of them next time you're in London at Simpson's over steaks and Château Lafite?"

"How right you are!"

"If you had to guess, what would you think Hodson might have done?"

"That's a *very* leading question and I ought to put down the phone. Actually, he could have done quite a number of things, but the really big sin against us would have been the private deal."

"What sort of private deal?"

"Well, our chaps get about. Suppose one of them is looking for Sheraton which some wretchedly impoverished member of the minor aristocracy is about to sell and he happens to see something tucked away in a dingy corner of the great hall which he is damn sure is another Rembrandt self-portrait. He goes back to London and puts in a report about the Sheraton sideboard but just fails to mention the Rembrandt. Get my drift?"

"You mean he arranges some kind of art black market sale?"

"It has been known to happen. And even a suspicion that one of our men might have been up to that little game means not only that he is out, but also that the word goes to our rivals and he's out of the legit business for good. We're strict about these things amongst ourselves, for the aforementioned reasons."

"Which doesn't necessarily mean he is out of the illegitimate business?"

"Well, yes and no. He might pull off one or two or even three private deals, but we'd all be watching him like a hawk all the time. We have our own security system to keep tabs on the bad boys, which is probably why most of us are so holy. Mind you, I'm not suggesting for one minute that Hodson was dealing on the side; I haven't a clue as to what put him under a cloud. He might have been rude to an Arab oil sheik. That's absolutely forbidden, too. It could even be that he just wasn't pretty enough for the job, in spite of his knowledge of painting. We like our chaps to be highly presentable. My wife married me for my beauty and it has stood me in marvelous stead, even outside of business. I was never mugged in America and we had an apartment for two years right on Central Park. Practically an all-time record. Jane says I was immune because the thugs all thought I was an out-of-work British actor specializing in those eccentric-Englishmen parts which no one is writing into their plays anymore."

The Honorable Jeffrey paused to get his breath, then went on.

"I don't know what's in your mind, Harris, but let's get one thing absolutely clear. Hodson's report on your Arran mock-Renoir has to be dead straight. Even if he'd wanted to, there was nothing he could do about that. You see, the letter requesting the visit of our expert from Lady something-or-other is on file in our London offices, along with Hodson's report, which was read to me. It's a very definite report. He said he couldn't make up his mind whether the painter had been trying to copy a Renoir for sale as such, or trying to suggest that his painting was an unrecorded original. He inclined to the view that it had been a straight copy of a section of 'La Galette,' but the hack had got bored with Renoir's placing of the people, shoving them about a bit."

"If it was a straight copy, why didn't he copy the whole thing?"

" 'La Galette' is big, very. The copier may have felt he wasn't up to the huge task, tiring quicker than Renoir. Also, smaller jobs widen the market amongst buyers. But the really important thing in all this is that Hodson identified the canvas as a twentieth-century product; something about the finishing, I don't know. That's how he dates your lady's painting as 1910 or later. Renoir simply couldn't have used that type of canvas; it wasn't available. That answer all your queries?"

"Just about."

"You still don't sound convinced."

"It's the quality of the painting."

"Look, copiers are sometimes real artists. They can paint. Especially when they have the work of a master right there in front of them. He was probably busy in the Louvre for weeks. You can see them at it. It's a minor trade. The thing is you must identify your copy and it is very naughty to put Renoir's name onto your work. Which your lady's copier did *not* do. Hodson's report said no signature, is that right?"

"Yes."

"Take my advice, old boy. Relax. Enjoy your holiday. But first tell me one thing. You don't collect now, but I've a hunch you did once. What?"

"Chinese pots."

"I *knew* it! Cancel that invite for drinks and come here for the night. Give you a pheasant for your dinner. And my cellar is made up of odd bottles from some rather nice vintages. Not the best, but a helluva sight better than you're likely to get up here anywhere else. Trade perk, really. How about it, eh?"

"It's extremely tempting, but I'm not setting up an agency for Harwell-Speed in Singapore."

"Not an agency. Just some fun and games for your spare time. I'm sure you need an outside interest."

"There are no bargains about these days in Singapore or Hong Kong or where you like. Everyone's too knowledgeable."

"My dear chap, we're not running an antique business. It's collections we want to learn about. You know . . . a mandarin or a towkay or whatever you call them who is just about to join his revered ancestors, who has collected Tang horses as a hobby but whose relations are all philistines and don't give a bugger about Tang anything. A word in their ears at the right moment of deep grief could see the whole collection shipped to Harwell-Speed for disposal at maximum price. Get me?"

"Too damn well. And I'm not doing it."

"I still want to warm your belly with good food and drink before a little chat. Coming?"

"All right; thanks."

"When?"

"I may be on Arran a few days more. I'll give you a ring."

"Do that. Incidentally, we have about thirty directors on our board. I'm one of them. We could make you another in Singapore. The fee isn't much but the commission's lovely."

"I'm already the chairman of three companies."

"Just what we need. That or a good title. You don't happen to have a Far Eastern decoration? Something like the Nineteenth Order of the Imperial Cherry Blossom?"

"That's about the last thing I'll ever get."

"Oh. Pity. See you. What's your phone number there?"

I told him and then went to sit alone for fish in the dining room, served by a George who never spoke, watching the cars drive up for the evening's boozing. These included a Land-Rover. Music was switched on and there were voices. My European meal this evening offered a package whipped pudding that hadn't been whipped; there were pink lumps in it. I skipped coffee and went into the bar.

Aishah was behind it, serving drinks, presumably because George was in the kitchen washing up my dishes. She was wearing red trousers and a pink chain-store blouse that rather suggested a *baju,* buttoned up to the neck with ruffles there and more ruffles on the cuffs of long sleeves. She had put on enough makeup for a Sungei Patani prostitute bound for the *ronggeng* dance, but in spite of this had no eyes for the male customers, apparently just ears for an old Beatles number on the tape. She didn't look at me. The major did, and though he didn't actually turn away, he partially averted his head. I went over.

"Evening. Join me in a malt?"

"I have a drink, thanks."

He was sulky. I asked Aishah for two malts. She swiveled and put a practiced hand on the right bottle when I named the brand, pouring without lifting her head. She took my money, replaced the bottle, fed the cash register, putting change on the counter, not noticing when I shook my head and left it. She left it, too. I set the second malt at the major's elbow and he gazed at it for a moment before breaking down.

"Thanks. I hear you've been visiting Lady Eloise?"

"Yes."

He lifted the glass. "Why didn't you say you know her?"

"I don't. My father did."

"You didn't come to the island just to see her?"

"Why should I? And what's it to you?"

That flustered him. He began on a cover-up for curiosity, which included a picture of happy island life that didn't exactly mesh with what he had been saying earlier about Arran, everyone popping in and out of each other's houses with the easy camaraderie of a small town in the Midwest of the States, the striking exception to this being Tigh-na-Claddach, where no one popped in. They didn't have an annual drinks party, that basic essential for community living. The major played golf with Angus quite frequently, but even when their game was on the course at the north end of the island Angus had never asked his partner home for drinks afterward. The major's lady's verdict on Anne, after one contact, had been that she didn't seem very womanly somehow.

The major was now sinking into the bog of the topic he had raised, acutely aware of this, and, like the hero of the old-type boys' adventure story, suddenly freed himself by one mighty leap, changing the subject.

"Do you fish?"

"Not really."

"What's that mean?"

"I've sat in boats with people, holding a rod. But what happened to them didn't happen to me."

The phone bell rang in the hall.

"Like to sit in a boat again? On an Arran loch? I have the rights. It's brown trout. We'll take the catch home and you can meet the wife. Mind you, we mayn't get much. Not the weather. All this heat. Fish don't rise."

The phone bell had stopped. George poked his head around the door to the bar and signaled me. I knew who was calling before I picked up the receiver.

"Anne Kennet. I'm sorry to bother you. Have I interrupted your meal?"

"It's over. And not memorable."

After a moment she said, "I hate to think of you in that place."

The telepathic exchange was in operation, all right.

"I rang because Mother's being a bit troublesome. And I thought she might ring you. She wants *me* to take her to London now, with the picture. I've refused, of course. The idea's crazy. It would be an absolute waste of money we can't afford. And she'd insist on going the rounds of the salesrooms. She just hasn't the strength for it."

"You're expecting another bid to rope me in for escort duties?"

"Yes. I thought you'd better be warned."

"Thanks. I won't give her any encouragement."

There was a pause.

"It might be best not to see her again. Even if she asks you to come here."

"All right."

The pause was even longer.

"Are you staying on the island for a while?"

"Maybe a few days. I've been asked to go fishing."

"Who with?"

"Major Henderson-Pratt."

"Oh. You realize that's going to mean hearing all about Chatmagundi back in the good old days?"

"I know. But it gets me out of this hotel."

"If you're staying on, you really ought to try to find someplace more comfortable. Would you like me to ask around? There's quite a good hotel at Corrie."

Only a mile or two from Tigh-na-Claddach.

"I'd like that."

"If I can't get you in the hotel, some of the houses take in people. I have a daily help who lives in Corrie. I'll get her onto this."

"I'm beginning to feel really looked after."

Another pause.

"It's just that . . . I'd like to talk to you again. About Malaysia."

"I know. We have that in common."

"Yes. Well . . . good night, Paul."

"Good night, Anne."

I hung up and stood for a moment with my hand still on the replaced receiver, as though by some nonelectronic magic this still maintained the connection. I went back into the bar. There must have been some change in my expression, for the major stared at me.

"Not bad news, I hope?"

"No. Not bad news."

FIVE

Hendy arrived to collect me at the hotel just before eleven, nearly an hour late. I had the feeling his wife didn't let him out until he had done the housework.

"We'll go in my Land-Rover. Last bit's over a rough track. Need something built for the job."

The Land-Rover may have been built for the job fifteen years earlier, but the best of machines wear out and this one had. Hendy seemed extremely proud of the seven forward speeds and three astern, or whatever it is these things possess, and kept running through the gears with teeth-jarring jerks and most unpleasant noises from the big end. As well as demonstrating the flexibility of his vehicle, he had to keep talking about it, shouting at me over engine noise all the way through Lamlash, then Brodick, then up the east coast road. Behind us a huge load of gear rattled and bounded.

We reached the point from where we were to start walking. A dirt road leading off the highway had become a track with grass down the middle, finally ending up as a rumor that cart wheels had come this way for peat cutting sometime last century. We climbed down and Hendy lowered the back, starting to pull things out—waders, fish baskets, lunch basket, two rods, oars, oarlocks, a heap of black rubber, and a pump to inflate it.

"You bring your own boat?"

"Have to. There isn't one on the lochan. Could fish from the shore all right, but I like getting out on the water."

"Where the hell is this water?"

He pointed up. Those mountains with black broken teeth growing out of gray gums were going to be hanging over me again. Hendy was fair about sharing the load. All I had to carry was the dinghy and pump, one rod, my lunch, and the waders; he took everything else. We started over ground still soggy from the last rains, what Hendy called machar, but I call swamp, the going really rough until we started to climb; then it was just a test of wind. Above rattles and clinkings I could hear my host breathing like a man who has had two coronaries with a third imminent. He was purple when the ground flattened out, but his eyes gleamed as though just ahead were all the joys of this world.

What I saw was a flat piece of bog presided over by those mountains and some water about the size of a successful Hollywood producer's swimming pool. But the sun was shining and grouse did their overloaded takeoffs under groaning engines. Until we started to make shore camp, that was the only noise breaking a most exquisite deep stillness. The view was pretty good, too, about a sixth of Scotland, water broken by islands of assorted sizes. A cargo ship down in the estuary was a toy.

Hendy wasn't interested in views; he was right in the middle of his big substitute for all the military campaigns in which he hadn't fought, inflating our assault boat. When this was ready I rolled up my trousers—there was only one pair of waders—to help launch it, momentarily worried about leeches until I felt the temperature of that water, in which no leech could have survived for five minutes.

"Pity about the sun," Hendy said.

Like all fishermen, he was readying his excuses early.

We spent the first hour with me being taught how to go about

74

landing brown trout, in whispers, with every now and then ringed bubbles breaking surface: fish laughter. The next hour was dedicated to Hendy's serious, totally silent attendance on his rod, with me holding mine for the look of things, but in spite of a special fly on my line nothing happened. Hendy didn't catch anything either. After that we made for shore base and lunch.

It was pleasant on land. We were in a heathery patch not at all damp and I lay back with that fragrance all around which is not unlike the scent of fresh straw matting in a Japanese country inn. The grouse had accepted us and were quiet, but there was now a hum of bees. Early days in India weren't too hard to take in these conditions and I lay listening, mostly with my eyes shut. Then, when Hendy went silent over opening a can of beer, I opened them. After a moment I said:

"You've paid your subscription for the right to fish here?"

"Eh? Why?"

"Someone's quite interested in us. Watching from that ridge up there. I caught a glint as he moved binoculars once or twice, but I think he's pretty steadily focused down here."

Hendy didn't seem to like this news much, reacting to it rather as he might have up on the Afghan frontier when attached to the Bengal Lancers, his head coming round very slowly. It was practically two minutes before he said anything.

"Keeper checking on the deer, I'd say."

"I don't see any deer."

"They're about. Bird-watching tourists and hikers and so on disturb the herds."

A gun banged.

"What's that?" I asked.

Hendy took a minute to decide.

"Hill farmer out after rabbits."

The noise had come from something of much heavier caliber than a shotgun. Two more bangs close together confirmed this, the echoes being batted about among deep crevices in the mountains the by-product of a sporting rifle. It was out of season for game birds and I hadn't seen a sign of rabbits up on this high grouse moor. I kept my eyes up on the ridge for any hint of a figure moving against the skyline, but saw nothing. Hendy got up.

"If we're going to have any trout for supper, it's time to get cracking."

"I've a feeling I'm a jinx on your fishing. I'll give you an hour or so on your own."

This didn't seem to hurt his feelings, and minutes later he was a picturesque figure beyond reeds, a wide-brimmed hat making him look remarkably like that static peasant sitting placidly in a boat so often used in Hokusai prints to suggest man diminished by nature. The mountains behind certainly diminished Hendy.

Two more shots disturbed the afternoon calm, but these seemed a lot farther away and after about half an hour I got up and began to stroll through heather down the gentle slope of the plateau, Hendy and his pond soon out of sight. To the west the ridge came down out of the mountains like a fat tree root going to earth. It cut off any view of Kintyre and the open Atlantic beyond and I was standing looking the other way, back toward Scotland, when the rifleman fired again. This time the echoes were preceded by a loud bee's buzzing not too far off my right ear. I was doing a free fall flat into heather when another shot put more buzzing to the left of me.

Heather doesn't offer much cover from higher ground unless you can really squirm down into it, but the patch on which I landed hadn't been burned off for years and kept me up on a pad of springy roots like the body in one of those ads for a double-innerspring mattress. The nearest area of decent rock cover was at least twenty yards away and in any run for it I would be almost as exposed as an antlered stag, without being nearly so fast over the distance. I stayed where I was.

Every year sees its human shooting casualties and it looked

as though I was about to start the summer tally of these when another shot put away the possibility, already remote, that I was the victim of an accident. This time the bullet hit the earth some four feet in front of my head, throwing up clods of peat through the scrub cover. A man up on that ridge, holding a rifle fitted with a telescopic sight, was boxing me in, first right, then left, then ahead. He was a marksman who got real pleasure out of his skill. If he had wanted to, he could have hit the target of my head with his first shot. Unless he was cat-playing with a victim, it looked as though I was being sent a message by a lethal form of hill telegraph. The message read that I wasn't wanted on Arran.

It was a bad five minutes while I waited to find out whether I had been talked to by gun. My heart told me how scared I was even while my mind stayed half anaesthetized by shock. Instinct said that if I ran for rock cover it might be tempting the gunman to do more than signal. For some time I could have been dead there in the heather. There were no more shots. The day returned to peace. Hendy might now have landed his first fish.

When finally I looked back at the ridge there was no sign of any movement among the rocks crowning it, but what I did see was pretty startling, a huge cloud wall going up for perhaps twenty thousand feet and moving east at speed, swallowing blue sky. I hadn't been chilled only by fear; there was a real temperature drop, fog pushing in front a forecast of its own cold. The torn peaks to the south were taken, one by one, then the ridge went. I stood up as the sun was eclipsed, beginning to run toward the lochan, reaching it just as Hendy, still out on the water, and moving his rod slightly, was taken.

I yelled to him to come out of there. His answer came baffled, and almost distant.

"Fish'll be rising now."

This was the way the world would end, not with fire, but in freezing fog, men isolated from each other, their cries blunted and padded off direction. Only on Highland lochs would be the occasional man in a rubber dinghy, or a leaking boat, missing the general panic because he was just about to land a brown trout.

I felt very lonely. Your first reaction to having been shot at is to tell someone about it as part of the recovery therapy, but I decided not to tell Hendy. I put on everything I had brought to wear and stomped up and down, beating my arms to keep circulation going. It was more than just winter suddenly. The Gulf Stream had gone off course and Scotland was about to develop an ice covering. I heard the slosh of oars and shouted:

"Catch your fish?"

"No. Still with our gear, are you?"

He found me by some sixth instinct and together we set about getting the dinghy out of the water, deflating it, and loading up for portage, not even an oarlock lost.

I don't know how we got down that hill. I bumped along just inside the visibility circle between us, Hendy encouraging me every twenty yards by saying that the fog would be thinner down in the glen. It wasn't, but he located our transport and took the time to pack in all the gear as carefully as a housewife stocking a deep-freeze. I left him to it and went to sit in one of the three front seats, shivering. There was no use putting on the engine and the heater blower; this Land-Rover had been commissioned before car heaters were invented. Hendy peered in at me.

"We get these sometimes. Heat fog."

He sounded positively cheerful, just the man for an Everest expedition which has chosen the wrong season for the ascent. A pup tent pitched on a glacier at eighteen thousand feet, with the wind at a hundred and ten miles an hour, and a couple of yeti roaming around outside growling, would really bring out the best in Hendy, making him merry as hell while he pumped the Primus to brew snow tea.

He settled in behind the wheel.

"Going to try driving in this?"

"We'll have a bash."

That was a pretty good forecast of what was to come. I hung out my side to warn us off the really big rocks, sure we were going to land in the burn instead of hitting the track, but the ruts began and in a kind of triumph he put speed up to five mph.

"Practically home and dry," he said.

We weren't quite. He miscalculated the steepness of the final gradient up to the highway and, with engine racing, did quite horrible things to the gearbox. There was a loud and ominous noise. He yanked on the hand brake. In that white chill he was sweating.

"Stripped a gear?"

"Feels like it."

"Sounded like it. How many?"

"I can't get anything but top. No use on this slope."

"Then stop revving! I'll put stones under the wheels."

When I climbed back into my seat, he was sitting slumped forward with his eyes shut. If this had been an Army vehicle operated on taxpayer's money, Hendy would have met the situation with a cheery quip, but the thought of civilian garage bills ahead was making him feel sick.

"What now?"

"She'll have to be towed." It was a moment before he added, "The road's up there."

"So we walk?"

"I have to stay."

"Why?"

"There's two hundred pounds' worth of stuff in the back. And this is the tourist season."

"You think there'll be a lot of tourists driving around this afternoon?"

"The fog could lift. I've got to stay."

"You want me to go off to the nearest phone?"

"Yes. It's downhill all the way to Sannox. If you stick to tarmac you can't go wrong."

"How far?"

"About three miles. Phone Macdonald's garage in Brodick. They're the only ones with breakdown gear."

Hiking in the fog on Arran is probably a lot better than hiking in the fog on a motorway; you're in no danger of being hit from behind by a rubber-wheeled freight train. But it was still eerie. The wind which must have driven that huge cloud bank had gone, as though with mission accomplished it had just given up, and the mist didn't drift, it felt static, a heavy stillness hung with gray moisture particles. The grouse were now all grounded and at this time of year sheep were too far along in parenthood to bother about sending out bleats for lost lambs. Sounds were the ones I made, mostly the whispering of my composition soles on the damp surface of the roadway. I share a sailor's loathing of fog and moved at only half speed ahead, contained in a visibility circle of about six feet, this just enough to keep me on asphalt and off the grass edging which rolled over into drainage ditches.

I was beginning to see liver spots in front of my eyes when a stone clinked on the roadway somewhere behind. I stopped. A sheep could have done that climbing up onto a heat-retaining hard surface, but there should also have been the faint click of hoofs. I stood waiting for something to come looming out of the fog, but nothing did. All I heard was my heart on overtime.

Then there was more sound, from up in those mountains, a rumble like an old volcano reactivating itself, this followed by a crash that could have been a regiment of artillery firing on signal. A second thunder salvo was introduced by a yellow flash through the gray. Rain came, a sound track turned up full. I walked fast, not bothering now about the visibility. The road-way became a stream. I had dressed sensibly for a summer's day in the hills—a Norwegian string vest, wool shirt, cashmere pullover, all topped off by a tweed jacket—but in a couple of minutes I was a moving test for fabric shrinkage under extreme conditions. I had no cap and water streamed down my neck from flattened hair in such a torrent I could practically feel the effects of erosion on my spine.

At least I was reprieved from that listening through silence and I began to run, jog-trotting, risking a spill on the slippery surface. I was in a skid toward a drainage ditch when I saw wire fencing with trees beyond it. The plantation had hung onto heat from earlier sun, pushing back fog, and it was easy enough to follow that netting around to Tigh-na-Claddach's barred gate. I didn't go through it at once, standing for a good five minutes looking at the highway, which was now almost all within my vision. Nothing came down it, and all I heard was the sea.

Rufus reacted to my ringing of the bell long before Anne did. Then I heard her telling the Baskerville cur to be quiet. I was inspected through a three-inch opening.

"Paul! Where on earth have you come from?"

"A great day's fishing."

The joke was mine, I should have appreciated audience reaction, but it went on a bit too long. While she laughed, I stood out in the rain like a clothed centerpiece for an Italian fountain under a water-pressure cut, not sending out those jets, just dripping.

"Oh . . . come in."

And about time, too. A moment later I was flooding tiles, with Rufus sniffing at my trousers.

"A hot bath for you. And a whisky."

"I've left my comrade up in the mountains. I must phone Macdonald's breakdown service. Hendy's Land-Rover's kaput."

"I'll do the phoning. Take off those shoes and come upstairs."

I left damp footprints on parquet and uncarpeted treads. In the bathroom Anne turned on the hot tap.

"I'll get you dry things of Angus's."

The dog was still sniffing at me, but Anne pushed him in front of her and shut the door. I put all my clothes in the washbasin and was sitting in hot water when she came back with the whisky, and no bourgeois politeness about knocking, either, but straight over to set the glass on the loo lid where I could reach it. Then she looked at me.

"Where is the major?"

"About three miles up the road on your left."

"I'll fetch him in the Mini."

"I wouldn't. Just phone and leave him there."

"Not a kind man, are you, Paul Harris?"

"That's right. Besides, you'd never get all his gear into your little box. And he's guarding it."

"We'll salvage what he values most."

She collected up the things in the washbasin on the way out. Minutes later, while I was still lying back in hot water, brooding, I heard a car going down the drive at a speed which showed no respect at all for fog. Hendy was certainly going to accept Anne's invitation to make his debut in this house. I do all my most useful thinking in deep hot baths, but I couldn't afford to linger in this one.

Angus's play trousers, a natty pink check on a yellow base, were too short in the leg and too roomy around the waist. I didn't like his shirt, semifloral, and a yellow sweater did nothing for me at all. The slippers were a size too big and when I flapped downstairs in them a shut-away Rufus protested.

There was a bright fire in the sitting room, but I didn't linger, going to the windows for a look over sodden grass toward the dak bungalow. Lady Eloise had a light on, needing this in the gloom behind those shrouding verandas, and as I was turning away I noticed a pair of binoculars on a chest, handily placed for bird or mother watching.

Anne's kitchen had been the last word in 1920, with not much done to it since except for the addition of a refrigerator. From it a stone-floored and chill passage led to a back door, which opened onto a courtyard entirely covered by cement that looked as if an earthquake had cracked it. Opposite was a double garage with rooms built above, the kind of accommodation for staff you could get away with forty years ago, with access by an outside stair. I did a dash through the rain to this and up, finding an open padlock hanging on a staple by the door.

There may not have been the money to modernize the kitchen, but Angus hadn't stinted himself when it came to power tools for his workshop. Above the bench a new skylight had been fitted and near a lathe was what looked like the beginnings of a footstool. In the middle of the floor sat a half-finished cabinet, professional enough work, with about half its veneer glued on, and an occasional table requiring its fourth leg, all this suggesting that the man who used this place got bored easily, starting a new project before finishing the old. The place clearly escaped routine domestic cleaning, though the floor appeared to have had a casual sweep recently, leaving a heap of wood shavings under the workbench. An old wardrobe with its door hanging open contained expensively bagged golf clubs, a golf cart, and what looked like old camping equipment rammed into a plastic bag. Angus also kept some of his personal reading matter over here, a couple of manuals on home carpentry and a paperback titled *Teach Yourself Karate*, this well illustrated.

The second room was used as a store, full of trunks and suitcases, plus odd pieces of old furniture obviously bought for the wood, some of it half sawn up. The light from one dirty window was poor but I saw a label on a cabin trunk that spoke to me of home: *Raffles Hotel*. I'm not sure what made me spin around then, I don't think I actually heard anything, but when I got back into the workshop the door to the stairs was open two inches. I was sure I had shut it. I had to weave about amongst the clutter to get to that outside landing. The stairs down were empty. There was no wind, rain falling straight, drumming on a slate roof and gurgling through rones. Then I did hear something, a car engine.

I was in a chair by the sitting room fire and holding up a paper when Hendy's voice came ringing from the vestibule, explaining that his oilskins had kept him quite dry. This was followed by more of the obsequious gratitude with which he must have been boring Anne all the way down the hill. He might have been knocked down by royalty and taken back to Buckingham Palace for bandaging and a wash. That was all he wanted, a quick wash. Anne came around the door and stopped to look at me.

"Rufus was making a lot of noise as we drove up. He doesn't usually bark at cars. Was it the phone?"

"No. He just wanted in here. All dogs love me."

She came across the room. "You might at least have put a log on the fire."

"I'm shy about taking the initiative in other people's houses. How did you locate Hendy?"

She tossed on a log, then another, her figure staying tight and firm in that telling bend-over test.

"I drove with the window down and he shouted when he heard the car."

"He was taking a big risk. You could have been a tourist out pinching rubber dinghies."

She straightened and looked down. "I get the impression somehow that things aren't going as you'd hoped?"

"They never do," I said.

Hendy arrived, rubbing his hands, his eyes flicking around the room so he would be able to describe it later to his wife. All he wanted was the smallest whisky and water, which surprised me somewhat. Perhaps he was trying to make it plain that if the Henderson-Pratts were ever asked here to drinks it wouldn't be too expensive for their hosts. He then became the life and soul of our threesome, not really too good at it, making the mistake of thinking that any girl would be fascinated by the romantic life he had led trying, unsuccessfully, to keep vertical the last props of crumbling empire. The only thing he spared us was Poona; he didn't seem to have been to Poona.

About the time we should have arrived with fish for his wife to fry, Hendy decided that he must phone her and would it be too much trouble? He did this within earshot, making it quite plain to Mrs. Henderson-Pratt just where he was, that the fortress of Tigh-na-Claddach had at last been breached, and I knew he had been asked whether Lady Eloise was one of our party when he said, "No, she's not here, dear."

"The rain's stopping," Anne told me over Hendy's noise in the hall.

I turned my head to look. "There isn't a cloud system anywhere that could go on with that rate of discharge, even the Indian monsoon."

She stood for cigarettes on the mantelpiece, put one in her mouth, but took it out again to start laughing.

"Have I missed a joke?" Hendy asked from the doorway.

"I'm afraid so," Anne said. "But it doesn't bear repeating."

"Well, in that case perhaps I can tell another?"

"By all means do. Paul needs cheering up."

Hendy had to make a second phone call, this time to Macdonald's garage. He came back into a sitting room Anne had left, looking gloomy. Apparently Mr. Macdonald had stated very plainly that he wasn't coming out in this muck and that the Land-Rover would be safe left unlocked in any car park in Europe, even with its gears functioning. It was the kind of impudence you were having to take from the natives all the time these days. The garage man was almost certainly a secret card-carrying member of the Scottish Nationalists. You never knew where you might run into them; that girl with the sweet smile in the chemist's shop could be one, even the man in the deerstalker on the ferry who looked as though he had at least five generations of Tory tradition behind him.

"You're to help yourself to another whisky," I said.

"Is Mrs. Kennet away getting supper?"

"I don't know. She just left."

"But really, Harris, do you think we ought to stay?"

"You don't have to. You could get a hire car to take you home."

"You're staying?"

"I have to. My trousers aren't dry. And our hostess doesn't like the idea of my wearing her husband's back to my hotel."

"Well . . . in that case . . ."

He sat down without even looking at the whisky. I sipped from my glass.

"How much time does Angus spend on Arran?"

"What?" Hendy appeared to be startled out of his own thoughts. "Oh, every weekend."

"Does that mean Friday to Monday?"

"Sometimes he stays over till Tuesday. I've golfed with him on a Monday."

"Where is this garage?"

"Just south of Largs. Quite near the ferry. Why?"

"I'd have thought the weekend the busiest time in that trade."

"You mean he ought to be there? I think he has a very good foreman."

"Who does all the work?"

"Oh, I wouldn't say that. Angus is on the car-selling side. It gets him about a good deal on the mainland. What is all this, Harris?"

"Curiosity."

The phone rang in the hall. It was answered quickly, but the door was shut and I couldn't hear anything. Hendy prowled around the room, all his stories too good to be served just to me as the audience. He might also be uneasy about taking a free meal off the Kennets at this stage in a developing relationship. I turned my head to see him standing at the French windows with the binoculars lifted and obviously focused on the dak bungalow.

"You could get in jail for that."

He started. "Eh?"

"Peeping Tom."

"My God, Harris, what do you mean?"

He put down the glasses with a bang. A shower of sparks shot out from flaring logs onto a rug already pitted with burn marks, the sharp cracks rather reminiscent of rifle fire.

"See if there's a screen someplace," I said.

I was stamping on red embers when there was a long, sharp cry from the front hall. I left Hendy to deal with a fire hazard.

Anne was standing just inside the vestibule, facing me, her face in shadow, a backdrop of whiteness behind her. She had her hands lifted in a curious, helpless gesture of appeal.

"It's Mother! She's . . . !"

Anne turned and ran out onto gravel. We reached the rose beds together. Lying among well-tended bushes, almost face downward on very wet ground, was Lady Eloise Martin-Macintosh. Her hat had been knocked askew, her head was within inches of a low stone wall edging the lawn. One hand, white-gloved, was clawed into the ground amidst a scattering of pink petals. Near her was an overnight case and half under her body a thinnish brown paper parcel about three feet square, tied with heavy cord.

Anne turned a stricken, terrified face.

"I didn't touch her! I think . . . she's dead!"

SIX

Lady Eloise was not dead. I turned her over gently, then half lifted her on one arm. Bits of well-weeded soil clung to her hair and there was a slight ooze from one corner of her mouth. I wiped this away and she moaned.

Hendy arrived. In a crisis he was neither comic nor a bore. There was a drill for casualties and he put it into operation at once, ordering Anne back to the house for a travel rug.

"We'll get her on the walk first," Hendy said. "Can't be anything broken. Ground's very soft."

"Old bones are brittle."

"Hold her up a bit more."

He did the physical while I took a pulse rate. Eloise's heart was still very much at it; I didn't even pick up a flutter. Hendy's assessment was brisk.

"Twisted an ankle on the walk. Fell. Fainted."

I had no comment. Before we could begin to lift Eloise, Anne was back with the rug, trembling as she helped us wrap an old woman in tartan.

"You want her up at your house?" I asked.

She nodded.

"Then get a bed ready and start filling hot-water bottles."

Anne left us again, running, but she was in the front hall waiting by the time we had finished the carry across gravel. The door to a downstairs bedroom was open.

"In here," she said.

Her gardener's tan had been undermined from beneath. Breathless, she seemed to find words difficult. Shock ought to have been wearing off by this time; fear is more lasting. Hendy and I laid Eloise on top of the bed. Anne just stood there, doing nothing, staring down.

"Hadn't you better get her out of those clothes? Have you phoned the doctor?"

"No."

"I'll do it," Hendy said.

I lifted Eloise again so that Anne could ease the old woman's arms out of the suit jacket.

"Have you any idea where your mother was going?"

She folded the jacket carefully, a chain-store heather mixture treated with the respect a Givenchy might have rated.

"It's crazy!"

Her fingers had found bumps in the jacket pocket and she began to pull things out—a wallet, purse, a comb, passport, bits of makeup. Eloise hadn't been able to carry a handbag.

"Where was she going?" I asked again.

Anne had been putting the articles from the pockets on a bedside table. She draped the jacket over a chair back.

"The last ferry for the mainland."

"How do you know?"

"She'd hired a car. It was to come to our gates and wait for her there. So I wouldn't know anything about it. But the ferry was canceled. Fog. The hire garage in Brodick rang the cottage to tell her, but there was no answer. So they rang me, just now."

"Do you know how long they'd been ringing your mother?"

"They'd tried three times. On and off for three-quarters of an hour."

"So she may have been lying in that rose bed for most of that time?"

Anne shook her head. "I don't think so. Mother's always early for everything. And she'd need at least half an hour to get from the cottage to the gate, carrying all this."

I looked at those swollen fingers. A kettle whistled in the kitchen. Anne swung around, wanting to get away from me. Even with her mouth open and her breathing loud, Eloise didn't look as I would have expected, old and sunk in weakness. Instead she might have been dreaming that she was accomplishing what she had set out to do, excited by success. I went out to collect a painting and an overnight case, on the way hearing Hendy at the phone.

"If he can come after office hours, that should be all right. We're getting her to bed."

The brown paper parcel wasn't light, but the weight of that overnight case should have made it a totally impossible lift for weakened hands. Eloise must have had to rest every few yards, setting down the suitcase and the parcel, then going through the laborious business of picking them up again, pain endured for a purpose, like parasol-holding.

Anne was coming down the hall carrying two hot-water bottles when I arrived with the luggage. I put the case on top of a bureau and the picture on the floor beside it. Anne came over with a key ring, almost brisk now, a lot of things to be done, finding a nightgown one of them. She unlocked the suitcase and lifted the lid.

There was a nightgown, all right, then a cardigan, and a plastic wash bag, but underneath, the rest of the space was given to carefully selected pieces of loot from a life out East— a silver jewel box, Siamese gold-inlaid hairbrushes, and fitted across these, with just room for it, that curved Malay kris from the bungalow's sitting room wall. The weapon's handle was set with stones that looked the real thing, the kind of gift a retiring British Resident would receive from a local rajah whose despotism he had fostered.

Anne stood staring into the case. She didn't say anything. She didn't need to. What we both saw did the talking. Eloise had been able to do what not many elderly people can—set off for a new life with very little clutter from the old, just a few pieces, the rest of what she needed to be bought in London when she had sold the Renoir. She would arrive on Mabel in Ootacamund with fresh equipment for the final phase, yesterday shaken off.

"I'll help you get her under the covers," I said.

"No! I can manage."

Hendy was in the kitchen making tea, curiosity dripping from him. I poured myself a cup, added milk and sugar, then sat down.

"Where on earth was Lady Eloise going?"

It wasn't my job to provide a cover story; the Kennets could do it.

"How should I know?"

"But what was in that parcel?"

"It hasn't been opened. Felt like a picture."

"A picture? What would she want that for?"

"Your guess is as good as mine. Suppose we leave it that Lady Eloise has had an accident in the garden?"

He got my meaning: no gossip at the ex-colonials' club. Three whiskies and the gossip would start, unless he saw himself as now in the Kennets' confidence, on the way to becoming an intimate at Tigh-na-Claddach. That would shut him up, but I didn't greatly care. I sat drinking tea, knowing that the sensible thing for me would be to catch the first ferry in the morning.

There was a screech from the bedroom, then words.

"I won't stay in this horrible house! I won't. Where's my picture? What have you done with it?"

We didn't hear what Anne replied to that, just a moment or two later her cry:

"No, Mother, no! Please!"

Hendy's chair scraped back. Seconds later we were both witnesses to the kind of scene that occurs often enough in the contemporary theater but that you don't often see in real life. Lady Eloise was out of the bed, on her feet, putting up a real resistance to Anne's attempts to get her back in among the hot-water bottles. An effort to put the old woman into a nightgown had apparently been abandoned and she was wearing scanties of black lace, the kind the ads practically guarantee as irresistible to a lover whose researches have already taken him that far. She wasn't modeling the set too well: a cleavage brassiere is a mistake when you're over seventy unless you've had plastic surgery in Hong Kong.

Our arrival wasn't really noticed, a serious and noisy contest going on between a possible contender for the world's lightweight ladies' septuagenarian title and her sparring partner, Anne looking as though she had already had too much. Eloise's thin arms were going like flails, clenched fists not contacting their target often, but every now and then there was a thump when they did. I had a quick look at Hendy, expecting to see him turning purple at the dreadful spectacle of the fair sex resorting to physical violence, but he was as calm as an experienced judge of holiday camp contests who already has a side bet on the winner he is going to choose. Suddenly age and a spell on damp ground told and Eloise sagged back against the bed, bare legs braced to hold herself up, mouth open, head down. We all just stood there until the old woman's head came up again. This time her gaze focused on me. She took a deep breath, then said:

"Get *out*, you *bloody* man!"

Hendy was the next target.

"Who is that *creature?*"

Maybe it was hurt pride that stung him into action. Hendy advanced.

"Lady Martin-Macintosh, you are getting back into bed!"

Eloise's reaction was feeble, as though sheer astonishment had winded her.

"Keep away from me!"

Hendy might have been a male nurse in a psychiatric ward; abuse from a patient meant nothing. He reached around behind her to push back the bedclothes, then flipped up her legs. She squealed as he pushed her down onto pillows and drew covers up to her chin, staying bent over the bed holding these in place.

"Anne! Get the police!"

Hendy remained punctilious about rank. "Lady Martin-Macintosh, I'm going to hold you like this until you stop making that noise."

Even in near hysteria Eloise was no fool. She looked up, hating her adversary, but realizing that she had to change tactics, trying a spell of an old woman's tears in a cruel world against which she is totally helpless. Hendy gave the act a full minute of his attention, then straightened and said gently:

"I expect you'd like a cup of tea? There's a pot brewed in the kitchen, Mrs. Kennet."

I went with Anne, leaving patient and therapist staring at each other. Anne put things on a tray, surprisingly composed for someone recovering from an assault.

"Do you have a lot of this kind of thing?"

She put sugar on the tray, not looking at me. "It's usually just words."

"Why do you put up with it?"

She poured milk into a jug. "It's the only interest we pay on a family loan."

The phone rang in the hall. Hendy jumped out of his chair like a highly paid private nurse determined not to have the patient disturbed, reaching the receiver before the bell had sounded four times. He kept his voice low, but I could still hear.

"Oh, it's you, Angus. Mrs. Kennet isn't here at the moment."

There was quite a long pause during which Angus might well

be asking what the hell Hendy was doing at Tigh-na-Claddach, and the explanation he got was complex, going on for a long time: fog, fishing, the Land-Rover. There was no mention of my part in any of this; it had been an army exercise.

"Yes. Lady Eloise has had a fall. That's why I'm still here. The doctor's on his way. We've put her to bed, but I'd say she's only suffering from shock."

Again the pause.

"I can't call your wife, Angus. She's over in the bungalow getting some things for Lady Eloise. Why don't you ring back later? Better wait until the doctor's been. He should be on his way now. Yes."

I put on a couple more logs, but they were green and hissed, so I got down on my knees with the bellows, pumping away, getting only sulky smoke from my effort. Hendy came around the door.

"Angus seems upset. I tried to tell him it wasn't serious."

"I heard you. Do you know where he was phoning from?"

"It would be the garage. There's no way he can get over tonight."

I stood up and walked past Hendy toward the hall.

"Where are you going?"

"To change."

My shoes weren't dry, but I took them anyway, the rest of my things wearable though the tweed jacket, pushed close to the kitchen stove on a chair back, was still heavy with damp. I changed in the bathroom, leaving the borrowed gear neatly folded along the edge of the tub. It wasn't easy to go down uncarpeted stairs without making any noise and Rufus heard me, whining from behind a bedroom door, but Hendy in the sitting room was using the bellows like Jove the windmaker. Log fires are great but you have to dedicate a large part of your living time to keeping them going.

I went through the kitchen and down the passage to the back door. Though the rain had stopped, the courtyard was still shining wet with puddles. I crossed over and climbed steps, but didn't go into the workshop, standing on the threshold looking at the floor. Faint damp traces of my feet propelling Angus's slippers were still visible, not a hint of new footprints made since my visit.

I didn't go back into the house, but walked out on a lawn like sodden felt. Everything dripped. Fog enclosed the estate, but the warm breathing of trees pushed it back, the lights in the bungalow quite bright, though the sea was completely hidden by a gray screen, and soundless, as though dead calm. I went over to the shore, pebbles mixed with sand that couldn't quite be called a beach, to find that the last tide had left an almost even line of multicolored seaweed, old rope, plastic detergent bottles, and a dead cormorant.

From here little probes of mist reached in toward the cottage, pointing up its isolation out on rocks, no place really for an old woman to end her days in, the accent on a loneliness that would certainly deepen during the glooms of winter. There is, too, an exclusive melancholy which attacks ex-tropic residents like Eloise when they are returned to source in a northern country. It wasn't just the loss of the pomp and ease which had once surrounded her, but physical as well. After thirty years in a sauna bath, the body's metabolism can never completely adjust to cold and damp, and from blood which refuses to thicken comes a kind of endless shivering in the mind. I had felt the first symptoms of this myself, but was always able to apply the cure, a plane East, and standing on that dank beach I could understand the reason for Eloise's wild rages. At Tigh-na-Claddach she felt already parceled for oblivion, even the escape device —her painting—no longer available.

The lights went out in the bungalow. Anne came across the lawn with two carryalls, one in each hand, hurrying, her head bent as though she was on a treacherous path where you had to watch your feet, but just before the paving through rose beds she stopped, putting down her load. She began searching for something, first along the low stone wall edging grass, following this away from me, then swinging back suddenly in my direction. She looked up and saw me.

There was more than twenty yards between us but a quality in that light seemed to define her face. It was set, rigid from anger at this invasion of what had always been a guaranteed privacy. I thought she was going to shout at me, but all she did was pick up the carryalls and hurry on through the roses toward gravel. There was the crunching of a car coming up the drive on dipped headlights. Anne went to meet it. I waited until she had taken the doctor into the house, then went to look where she had been looking. I found nothing.

I sat surrounded by gear salvaged from the Land-Rover, with a view of the back of the doctor's head, and his eyes and nose in the driving mirror. He was a small man, compact, dark, about forty, the age when medical idealism begins to wear a bit thin at the elbows. On the shore road the fog was still thick and he drove by what seemed to be some form of bat's sonar, interpreting sound echoes from steep slopes on one side, hitting a good thirty-five on bad bends and forty on the few straights, like a ship on radar which doesn't need to see where it is going. Instead of hanging out of his window to help with navigation, Hendy made small talk.

"I suppose a fall at her time of life means you're worried about complications?"

"No," the doctor said.

After an S-bend he added, "She'll die of old age, like three-quarters of the people on this island. As yet no reliable cure is available for the condition. And if some fool invents one, I hope it'll be suppressed."

Hendy thought about that for all of a minute. "You don't believe in people living to be old?"

"It's not a matter of belief. It's going to be sheer hell if too many of us do."

I could feel Hendy brooding then. The medical man on whom he might have to rely in an emergency didn't appear totally dedicated to the concept of preserving human life to its maximum limits. There was dead silence for some time, then the doctor broke it.

"Do you know where she was going?"

"Not really," Hendy said. "Except that she'd hired a car to take her to the ferry."

He had been listening from the hall.

"Planning to travel with that chopper in her suitcase?"

The doctor had sharp eyes as well as a chiseled tongue. Hendy was bolt upright in his seat.

"Chopper?"

"Yes. Some kind of Eastern short sword. The old girl is very proud of it. Had it down from the wall for me once. Still as sharp as a razor."

Hendy jerked his head around to stare at me. "Do you know anything about this?"

"Yes."

"Well?" the doctor asked, accelerating for a straight. "You don't usually take a jeweled-handled chopper away for a weekend. Where was she making for?"

"India. A place called Ootacamund."

The car went into another bend too fast.

"I see. That ought to make a nice change for her. Probably thinks Indian doctors'll do more than I can. Expects me to cure arthritis."

"Won't the climate out there help?"

"No climate will unknot those hands. Not even the middle of the Sahara. She'll never paint again. That's what's soured her. I believe she was once an internationally famous artist."

He might believe it; I didn't. It wasn't that an internationally famous artist couldn't have slipped through the net of my observation—I'm sure plenty of them have—just that the publicity about any painter operating out of Southeast Asia who had achieved even minor world celebrity would have reached me. My particular global area is almost totally dedicated to commerce, which leaves it a bit unpolished culturally, and there are moments when we feel slightly sensitive about this, so that on the rare occasions when we do produce a painter or a writer or even a poet who comes in for a nod or two from the larger world, this is pounced on with a great ho-ha in our press and elsewhere. Publicity of that kind doesn't cost anyone any money and it gives us a feeling that as well as being business whiz kids we are also a pleasantly civilized community; which was why I was dead certain that if Lady Eloise had ever sold a painting from a London gallery for twenty pounds she would have been proclaimed throughout Southeast Asia as Borneo's answer to Picasso.

We've only really had one painter for whom the trumpets have sounded with a modest noise in London, followed by half a fanfare in Paris and a tootle in New York—rather a mystery figure, called E. Kell. It has been suggested that E. Kell was a civil servant of the lower echelons, who sublimated career frustrations with rather savagely painted heads, just heads, Chinese, Malay, Dayak, one a pickled, decapitated head about which there was considerable interest and which sold for quite a lot of money to a private collector in Detroit. Kell's identity was never established, though all kinds of people looked mysterious when fingers were pointed at them, and it is now generally assumed that he died some time ago or that his muse deserted him when he retired on pension to the English south coast. At any rate, there have been no E. Kells for some time, and in fact there never were very many, perhaps three dozen at the most. I happen to know one quite well because Prince Batim Salong has it hanging in the reception room of his rococo palace just south of Kuala Lumpur. This is the head of a rajah painted with an arresting, harsh boldness, the subject arrogant, handsome, coldly intelligent, but with all that weak, which makes it an almost frightening portrait.

Batim got it in Europe while studying Western civilization—a two-year course which turned him into an alcoholic—and he claims he bought the thing because it reminded him of an uncle, a somewhat dangerous eccentric who ignored the twentieth century. The picture reminds *me* of Batim when younger, before fat added jowls to a sculptured profile. It is not a painting I would care to own or live with.

The doctor's personal angel got us alive to Brodick, where he left us to hurry off to a patient. Hendy deserted me, too, to get salvage operations started on the Land-Rover. I went looking for the supper that hadn't been served at Tigh-na-Claddach, finding a hotel which I think mistook me for a north end native on account of a general crumpled appearance and wet tweed. At any rate, they offered me fried fish if I didn't mind haddock, which I accepted, my voice as we discussed the menu betraying what I really was. But they stuck to contract and I ate in a huge room empty except for chairs, tables and sauce bottles, afterward driven back to Lamlash by a handyman for a fee which put me right back into the tourist category.

Window rattle woke me. We were experiencing another of those climatic changes which make life in Scotland so excitingly unpredictable—not a full gale, just a force six from the southeast. It would blow away the fog and tomorrow would be different. Dawn hadn't yet arrived and I was perfectly comfortable, the bed now friendly, three nights of me and hot-water bottles having dried it out, but I was still wide awake, as though a voice had called my name loudly. It wasn't a voice, it was my computer, hard at work while I rested and now ready with a conclusion from data I couldn't remember feeding in. Circuits had, of course, been activated by the doctor's information that Lady Eloise had once been an internationally celebrated painter, to which was then added previously stored facts on E. Kell. Answer: Lady Eloise was E. Kell.

I'm sure the conclusion wouldn't have been anything like so

definite if I had only had the one meeting with a Resident's widow, that performance under a parasol. The morning-coffee Lady Eloise could only have been a weekend painter, and in watercolors, charming little impressions of native life out East seen from a considerable distance and suitably idealized. But there had also been an old woman hitting out at an adopted daughter for whom she didn't even pretend to have any real affection. That old woman could have painted the rajah and the pickled head.

Immediately after breakfast I was in the Avenger, headed north. I would soon have this road memorized like a native, knowing which corners were lethal to take without a foot off the accelerator and which were only a major risk at over forty. It was sunny but not as warm as it had been before the fog, and I drove with all the windows shut and the heater on, reaching Tigh-na-Claddach at about half past ten.

The green Mini wasn't in the drive and there was no answer when I rang the bell. Rufus didn't bark. I began to walk around the house, looking in ground-floor windows, cautious when I came to the one behind which an old lady might be dozing. She wasn't in the bed, which had been made up. There was no sign, either, of her suitcase on the chest. I didn't think, somehow, that Eloise would have allowed herself to be moved upstairs, even if it was convenient for the bathroom, which meant that somehow she had been transported back to the dak bungalow.

The door from the veranda into the sitting room was unlocked. I made a quiet entrance. The Renoir was back on its nail and the kris hanging from its cords. I was stopped by a shout which held no hint of invalidism.

"Who's that?"

"The bloody man."

There was a twenty-second silence, then Eloise called out. "I'm in here."

She was sitting up in bed, with an invalid table braced across the covers like a last line of defense from which she could hurl things at an intruder. There was plenty to throw, too—a Thermos flask, a cup, a tin of biscuits, a book or two, and magazines. Above all this was the Dresden head, now haloed by curlers. Around her neck, restraining muscle sag there, was a white bandage which I thought at first was some part of a general beauty treatment.

"I didn't expect to see *you* again."

"I came to see how you were today."

"Did you? Well, I'm aching from my neck right down my back. Anne says I twisted my head when I fell. It feels as though I'd been hit with a flatiron."

"Swelling?"

"Anne says not. I don't know. What did you really come for?"

"Can I sit down?"

"If you must. Well?"

"Are you E. Kell?"

She stared at me for quite some time. "So *that's* it. You waited until you saw Anne leave, I suppose?"

"Not today. I've been ringing the bell at the big house."

"She's gone to meet Angus at the ferry. I won't stay up there when he's on the place. So I came back here."

Unless Anne had carried her, which seemed improbable, she had walked, which made her invalidism slightly overdone.

"You haven't answered my question, Eloise."

"I gave your father's son the right to use my first name. Not a ruffian who comes bursting into bedrooms."

"You haven't answered my question, Lady Martin-Macintosh."

"Why should I?"

"It could be very important. For you."

"What's important about being E. Kell?"

"I read about the last Kell painting that came up for auction. It fetched somewhere in the region of three thousand five hundred pounds."

There wasn't the slightest change in her expression.

"And you think I don't know about that?"

"It's reasonable that you shouldn't. The auction I'm talking about was in Singapore. The real market for Kells seems to be out East."

"How interesting."

"In spite of business doldrums they go on appreciating, which is the absolute reverse of every share I own. I wish I had bought one years ago. Maybe three."

Eloise was now looking slightly bored. "Do you?" she said.

She reached out for a Kelantan silver case, opened it, had a bit of trouble plucking out the cigarette, but managed this and to get her lighter working as well. She blew out smoke which had been sucked in deep.

"You imagined, Mr. Harris, that living on Arran I'd be right out of touch with everything?"

"You more or less said so yourself."

"I was not referring to the art world. I keep up my interest there. For obvious reasons. An E. Kell was recently sold in America for twenty-three thousand dollars."

After a moment I said, "Not the pickled head?"

"You know it?"

"Only in reproduction."

"My best work."

The statement rated a two-minute silence, but I gave it only about a quarter of that.

"I came here, Lady Martin-Macintosh, to suggest that if you have half a dozen E. Kells stored away somewhere, you can hang on to your Renoir but still go to Ootacamund without any fears about having to live on a friend's charity. That is, of course, if you don't mind selling your work?"

She smiled at me. "You came here, Mr. Harris, hoping to see a silly old woman's joy at the news that her paintings were still of value out in the world's marketplace. Were you ever a boy scout?"

"No."

"You should have been. You have the right instincts. The moral obligation to do good deeds regularly, once a day if possible. I'm so sorry to have spoiled the one for today. On the latest information, the market value of all my paintings stands somewhere in the region of ninety thousand pounds. As you suggest, the prices are keeping pace with inflation very nicely. The scarcity value contributes to that. I haven't sent out many paintings."

"The point is, how many did you keep? For yourself?"

"I came to that point long ago. The answer is none."

"You sold *everything?*"

"Everything that I thought ought to go out from my studio, yes. That is, when I became established. I was very lucky there. Like Renoir, I found myself a good agent, more by luck than anything else. Poor Arnold is dead now, but he did his work well. Though not as well as he would have wished."

"What does that mean?"

"He didn't like not being able to put his artist on display, along with her paintings. He did his best with the mystery of my identity, that kind of thing, but he kept saying it really wasn't good for business. I ought to be seen in London, Paris, and New York, and also develop wild eccentricities. He once suggested over lunch in the Café Royal that my price in the galleries would zoom if I shot Sir John, after which he would leak the news that the lady with the revolver was E. Kell."

Her laugh sounded a bit like a Peke's bark. There was not a visible trace of yesterday's ordeal in a rose bed. She didn't in the least mind my seeing her in her curlers, having decided that I didn't matter. She had been, however, bored in bed this morning, and was pleased to have an audience.

"Arnold was very much a man of these times, considerably before they hit us, which put him well out ahead. So I benefited."

"Why couldn't you let him publicize you in any way?"

"Aren't you forgetting that I was the wife of a British Resident? There was John's position to consider. All I could do was go back to Tetuan and paint the pickled head, as you are pleased to call it. Probably in frustration. Arnold was very pleased with it, saying it was just what he had been hoping for from me. He promoted me in America with that head. I estimate it put fifty percent on the price of everything I did afterwards."

"Surely you must have kept something for yourself from all this?"

"No. I destroyed what I kept back. It was second- and sometimes third-rate work. Bad Kell, in fact. Unlike so many artists, I was scrupulous about not letting these paintings be seen or marketed, I sold what I was certain was good Kell for the best price Arnold could get for me. We needed the money. His Majesty's Colonial Service in those days did not pay its servants enough to keep up the style expected of them. If you were to achieve the higher ranks you had to have some money of your own, the more the better. This was essential for promotion. The family money behind my husband was E. Kell. It would never have done to have it known that this money came from his wife's rather strange paintings. Had that got out, John would never have received his knighthood and he would not have been appointed to Tetuan."

"Do you mind if I sit down?"

"Why not, since I would appear to be giving a levee this morning?"

She poured herself a cup of milky coffee from the Thermos, sustenance for an invalid. I was not offered any. She sipped, looking at me.

"What do you feel about that Renoir now, Harris?"

"I don't understand."

"Surely you realize by this time that I'm a professional? And a professional can assess the work of another professional. Much better than some jackanapes from London who has set himself up as an expert. I knew that painting next door was a Renoir the first time I saw it and that is precisely what it is. I have only to take the picture to the National Gallery to have it confirmed, which will be the first step. I was about to take that first step yesterday after you had refused to help me."

"It's up to your family to help you."

"My family consists of a daughter by courtesy and the scoundrel she married. If that man had been an assistant to my husband on a Malayan station I'd have seen that he was sent packing. I dislike failures. And why shouldn't I? I was a success myself once. It didn't come easily. I painted for fifteen years with no recognition of any kind, a worry to my parents first, then something of a joke to my husband . . . until I started selling. Until Arnold believed in me, I was quite alone. I don't suppose you know what that feels like?"

"I've had some experience of being alone."

"Have you?" She stared at me. "What pictures of mine have you seen?"

"Four or five. The rajah often."

"I did three rajahs. If it is the one still in Malaysia, it must now belong to Batim Salong?"

"Yes."

"Then you know him well?"

"Yes."

"He collects?"

"No. Just your picture."

"I think I met him a few times when he was a boy. John certainly knew his father. So did I, slightly. Not a very intelligent man. What's the son like?"

"Very intelligent."

"I'm glad to hear it. I don't like fools to own my paintings. Tell me, what put you onto the fact that I was Kell?"

"Something the doctor said in the car going back to Brodick last night."

"And what might that be?"

"That you were an internationally known painter. There

haven't been all that many working from Southeast Asia, so it wasn't a brilliant deduction. Did you tell the doctor about your work?"

"I suppose I did, up to a point, though not that I was Kell. It must have been in a moment of frustration over these." She held up her hands. "I could still paint if I could hold a brush. I could paint you, Paul Harris."

"It wouldn't be one of the pictures you'd allow out of your studio."

She considered me as subject material.

"Oh, I don't know. You might be quite interesting. The man of principle in conflict with the man of expediency. With the expediency winning."

It was a nasty thing to say and too damn near the truth to be dismissed with a laugh. From Dresden china I was getting a gentle smile, only her eyes damaging the sweet-old-lady look. Renoir would have had a hard job idealizing Lady Martin-Macintosh, but then he wouldn't have tried to, women like this one not allowed into his painter's world.

Eloise turned her head, staring toward the door.

"So you're back, Anne? Mr. Harris very kindly called to inquire how I was. And now he has agreed to travel with me to London tomorrow. Isn't that kind of him? I realize I *do* need someone to help me."

SEVEN

Eloise was pleased with the effect of her shock assault, bright-eyed and ready for counterattack from either Anne or me, or both. Anne mounted this badly.

"Mother! You're talking nonsense! And you know it! You can't go to London! Mr. Harris isn't taking you anywhere!"

There was a silence then, during which I stood up.

"Isn't he?" Eloise asked. "What do you say to that, Paul?"

"Yes, I'll take you."

Anne turned to me almost slowly, an awkward pivot on her heels.

"But . . . you can't mean that. You told me you were going to the Hebrides."

"I've been going there for years. Somehow I never manage."

"Why should Mother stop you?"

Eloise answered. "Because I appealed to him for help. As his father's son."

She could deliver a ham line as effectively as any aging queen of the theater, control and timing perfect, making a nonsense seem credible. Anne's reaction did nothing to improve her tactical position.

"Have you *both* gone mad? Mother's not fit to travel anywhere!"

I had a feeling the doctor would play his part in helping to move Eloise to another continent.

"I am perfectly able to travel in a car. Which is what we'll be doing, isn't it, Paul?"

"Yes."

"Then it's all quite simple. An overnight stop in a hotel somewhere. In London I'll be staying at the Overseas Club. It may well take a few weeks to negotiate the sale of the Renoir and I'm hoping that Paul will be able to give me some help there, too. At least at the start."

I looked at Anne, remembering what she had said about Eloise's assaults being mostly verbal. This was one of them, a garden roller of words not even creaking as it flattened everything in front of it.

"You can help me to get ready, Anne. My big suitcases, I think, since I won't be carrying them this time. And there are some things I want to put in a trunk. For forwarding on to India later. I shall go by sea. A long voyage will be bracing and you can still get good service on a ship if you're able to pay for it."

Anne shouted, "You don't have a Renoir! And you *know* it! When are you going to admit that and stop all this madness?"

"Never." Eloise looked at me. "What ferry do you suggest tomorrow, Paul?"

"How about going today? The evening boat? We could take two nights on the way south, the first at the hotel at Turnberry. It has four stars."

Four stars appealed to her and it was a moment before she shook her head.

"No, I couldn't manage today, even with Anne helping me. There's a lot to be seen to besides packing. I'll have to arrange power of attorney for the estate with my Brodick banker, for one thing. I want to leave everything as tidy as possible for Anne."

"Mother! For heaven's sake . . ."

"If there's a boat about two, that should do us, Paul. At this time of year you sometimes have to reserve a place for a car."

"All right. I'll see about a booking on it and ring you when that's confirmed."

"Do. Until tomorrow, then."

I didn't look at Anne as I went out. While I was still in the sitting room, Eloise started to talk again. She might have been giving orders to a maid.

Walking through a garden that was a groomed and charming setting for the escape life, I began to have qualms about what I was doing. The willful old, like the young, shouldn't perhaps be treated as free agents, their dependence on others ruling against this. Eloise was, of course, only helpless in the physical sense, but she would have to be looked after until I could find someone else to take over, perhaps hire a temporary companion in London. I certainly wouldn't be able to leave her on her own until the value, or worthlessness, of that painting was confirmed. If Anne was right about the Renoir, then I was going to have a crisis on my hands, an old woman with her dream shattered, and I had no idea how I would cope with that. Against all this, though, was that sixth sense, by no means always reliable, urging me to get Eloise out of Tigh-na-Claddach as soon as possible.

I was on the path through the rose beds when Angus came out of the front door of the main house, with Rufus. The dog came bounding toward me, but was checked by a sharp, clear whistle from his master. Angus might live in a grace-and-favor residence by courtesy of his mother-in-law, but this morning he looked like a male model in one of those ads for expensive men's knitwear, the country house behind him, the dog obedient to his command, the good life his by right of generations behind him established in it. He was wearing well-creased slacks with a red stripe through them, and a scarlet turtleneck sweater. Tigh-na-Claddach had been more his idea than Anne's, I had no doubt. He took a brier out of his mouth to smile. "Been visiting our runaway, have you? How is she?"

"Seems fine this morning."

The smile widened. "She'll probably have a relapse if she sees me. I think I'll keep clear. Rather pointless my coming back, really. But Anne's been telling me what you did last night. Thanks."

"The major was in charge."

Angus laughed. "Hendy would love that. I'll pay my debt with a bottle of whisky. What's this about his Land-Rover?"

"I'd say it was a write-off."

"It has been for years. He'll be gloomy?"

"Very."

"I might help with a replacement. Trouble is, he has no money. Even for easy terms. And I'm not an accredited charity for tax purposes. Look, how about a game of golf? I can get you clubs. There's damn all for me to do here now the old girl's conscious. You'll have heard I'm not allowed in the bungalow?"

I opened the Avenger's door. "I'll skip golf, I think. I'm spending the day looking at bits of the island I haven't seen. I leave tomorrow."

"Back East?"

"After a time in London."

"I see. Well, I won't ask you to give my love to Kuala Lumpur."

I got in behind the wheel. Angus stood there with the house a backdrop, the dog a prop, a host seeing a guest off the premises. I turned the car toward the gates and he gave me a wave. In the driving mirror I saw Anne almost running across the lawn. She must have called out to Angus. He turned and went to meet her.

The man in the reception shed at Brodick harbor was as relaxed and slow-voiced as an old-time Texas sheriff in a movie, same chair tilted back against a wooden filing cabinet, same slow smile for the stranger, everything except the metal star and two guns. He didn't seem much interested in my plans to get back to the mainland next day; a lot of other people thought the weather was going to break, too, and had booked up the boat I wanted. He had a waiting list of twenty-three cars carried over from that ferry to the next.

"You could try Lochranza, mister. There's nae booking there. You just queue up."

I thought about taking my aged and arthritic passenger a long detour over devious Highland roads before we even reached Glasgow for the further four hundred miles to London.

"Mind you," the man in the chair said, "I've seen forty cars waiting all day up at Lochranza."

I found a phone box and dialed Eloise's number, not getting through; no busy signal, just a steady whine. I tried the main house at Tigh-na-Claddach and the bell rang, all right, but there was no answer. The exchange couldn't get me the number I wanted next from the information I gave them and I had to walk up to the post office. They knew all about Angus Kennet's garage on the mainland and made the connection for me, to a voice with a thick Ayrshire accent which sounded as though it was strained through a heavy mustache.

"Mr. Kennet's no here."

"I was to ring him yesterday or today. About a new car."

"Was you? He musta forgot. He's aye daeing that. I dae maist o' the business in this place. Can I no fix you up?"

"I think I'd rather deal with Mr. Kennet."

"Please yersel'." That was sour.

"Can you tell me how long he's been away?"

"Aye. A couple o' days. Awa' up to Inveraray wi' a job he hopes tae sell. It'll be a miracle if he can dae it. He might be back the morn. You can ring then."

My contact's receiver clicked down. I didn't need a map to tell me that Inveraray was well on the way to Kintyre and that back entrance to Arran at Lochranza, suddenly certain that wherever Anne had picked up her husband this morning, it hadn't been from a mini-liner arriving at Brodick. My heartbeat was well above normal as I tried Eloise's number again, getting the whine that means a phone out of order or disconnected. The Kennet bell rang for all of two minutes before a woman's voice which certainly wasn't Anne's said:

"What is it?"

"I want to speak to Mrs. Kennet, please."

"She's away."

"I've been trying to get the bungalow. The line seems out of order."

"I wouldnae know aboot that. But she's away, too."

"Who are you?"

"I oblige. Cleanin'."

"Then you must know where Lady Martin-Macintosh is?"

"Aye. Took to the cottage."

"I don't get that. The cottage?"

I was shouted at. "The cottage hospital!"

"You mean . . . she's ill? Worse after last night?"

"I dinny ken onything aboot last night. But she's had an accident today."

"What kind of an accident?"

"I only ken what they telt me. I'm just in afternoons frae Corrie. Mrs. Kennet was away in ambulance wi' the old lady as I got off my bus. It was him that telt me."

"Is Mr. Kennet there now?"

"No. He went aff in the wee car."

"Can you tell me your name, please?"

"What for?"

"I like to know who I'm talking to."

"Do you? Well, it's Wilson. *Mrs.* Wilson. And who may you be?"

"A friend of Lady Martin-Macintosh. The name is Harris."

"Well, I'll say you phoned. If they're back afore I'm away."

"Just a minute! What did Mr. Kennet tell you?"

"Eh? Oh, no much. Just that she fell affa chair. Don't ask me what an old body like her, and half crippled, was daeing up on a chair. I wouldnae ken. Is that all, mister? I've got my work."

The cottage hospital dated from the reign of Queen Victoria, updated with National Health additions. There were about a dozen cars in the parking area and one of them was the green Mini. I put the Avenger in a patch of shadow and got out to look at windows set high in the wall, like a nineteenth-century school, probably in this case so that patients wouldn't be distracted from making a good death by much of a view of the world they were leaving.

The Mini's driving window was down and the key in the ignition. I took it out and went to sit on a bench, a hospital reception area no place for a confrontation with the Kennets. I didn't have long to wait. Anne came out without Angus. She walked very slowly across the parking area, her head down. She was in slacks and a cotton shirt, her hair looking as though she had come from weeding rose beds in a high wind. She leaned on the roof of the Mini for a good minute before getting in. Seated, she put both hands up over her face, holding them there. It wasn't glare from poured concrete she was trying to shut away.

I didn't really know this woman, and yet her identity had invaded mine. I was so conscious of her now that I felt certain the potency of this would stab through her isolation in a personal crisis. She took her hands away from her face and quite slowly turned her head.

I got up from the bench. When I reached the open window of the Mini she was staring toward the hospital.

"Did your mother fall off a chair because you wouldn't help her pack?"

Anne said nothing. She reached out toward the ignition switch, her body bent forward, hair screening the side of her face, but she didn't actually touch the dashboard, her hand suspended as though the fingers were nerveless. She was sitting in that seat trembling. Then she saw there was no key. She spoke without looking at me.

"Give it to me! You've no right to anything of mine!"

It would have been a silly thing to say to anyone else. I gave her the key. She had difficulty getting it into the switch.

"How is your mother?"

"Ask them in there if you must know! If you hadn't said you'd take her to London . . . Why did you do that?"

"She was going to get to London anyway. Somehow."

"That's no answer!"

"It's half of one. Want the other half?"

"No! Just stay away from us! For God's sake stay away!"

The engine coughed twice, then fired.

"It's Angus you're afraid of, isn't it?"

Even that didn't make her look at me. She shoved in a gear and released the brake.

"Drive carefully," I said.

I watched it out of the parking lot, then a rattling progress down the drive to the gates. She swung the car toward Brodick town center.

There was no one in the hospital reception area, just a number of seated figures in a room to the left, labeled "Outpatients" —a girl defying the no-smoking notice as she jiggled a baby on her knees, an old man leaning forward on a stick, a middle-aged woman pretending to read a magazine, each little islands of self-concern on a row of hard seats. I was looking for a bell when a door opened down a corridor and a large woman glanced at me, then made a crackling advance, either a ward sister or the matron herself. Though she was starched to her cap, her face contradicted this formality, her manner authoritative but also humane. In this place she knew most of her patients personally. Sooner or later everyone would pass through her hands, most of them arriving in fear.

"Yes?"

"I came to ask about Lady Martin-Macintosh."

114

"She's as well as can be expected in the circumstances."

"Just what does that mean, matron?"

The woman smiled. "It means that she is under sedation for shock. She hasn't been x-rayed and we can't say yet whether or not her hip is fractured."

"If it is?"

"It will have to be pinned. An operation."

"Serious at her age?"

"Yes. But they're done all the time."

"On the island?"

"No. She'll be taken to Glasgow."

"If it has to be an operation, how long before she could travel?"

"Travel where?"

"London."

"Difficult to say. If everything goes well, she might manage in six weeks. But I doubt if her surgeon would want her to go far from home. She could be back on the island in a fortnight, though."

"I see. Thank you very much."

I was conscious of being watched as I turned away. She called out suddenly, "Is your first name Paul?"

I swung around. "Yes."

She came up to me, lowering her voice. "Lady Martin-Macintosh was asking for you."

"When?"

"For quite some time. Before sedation took effect. She kept saying, 'Get Paul.' Even when her daughter was there."

The matron didn't pretend not to be curious.

"Can I see her now?"

"There would be no point, at the moment."

"Then I'll come back."

"I'll tell her that when she's awake again."

"I was going to take her to London. That must have been in her mind."

"I see."

The matron sniffed, spun about on one heel, and beamed a very loud voice straight toward the outpatients' waiting room.

"Morag! You had eight years at school—you ought to be able to read! That no-smoking sign is staring straight at you!"

I went through the outer door and down the steps.

In the Far East I can usually assess to a pretty fine point just what inducement is called for to get someone to talk, but on Arran, and for a daily help who "obliged," I had no experience to guide me, deciding on a two-pound box of chocolates, for a starter at any rate. I had no difficulty in finding where Mrs. Wilson lived; it was up in High Corrie, a row of cottages on the hill behind a village straggling along the shore road. I went on foot, past hens cackling in the sunshine, barked at by a black-and-white collie, past an old man in heavy dark serge digging his garden who made a point of not acknowledging tourists, on to a young woman in a deck chair sunbathing who almost certainly wasn't a native, an unnatural blonde bold about large breasts in a minimal bra. I think she must have been asleep behind sunglasses, or at least had her eyes shut, for she sat up suddenly, jerking them off to stare at me. I was appraised and judged not wanting as a holiday contact, awarded a too shiny white smile.

"Mrs. Wilson? I think that's the last cottage. The one with all those geraniums."

They were pelargoniums, masses of them in all colors, some outside, others behind the glass windows of a small porch. A cat watched me go up the path, then went back to washing behind its ears. There was no bell. I knocked on an open door. Mince and onions were cooking somewhere at the back. I knocked again. An inner door filled first, then the outer.

Mrs. Wilson was suffering from a common Scottish ailment, starch heaviness. A round face above her fleshy body said nothing about leavening the burden of living by humor. Her mouth

was a line which separated when she spoke, then sealed up
again.

"Yes?"

"I'm Paul Harris. We spoke on the phone."

She had spotted the box under my arm.

"Aye. Well?"

It was not an island accent, pure Glasgow.

"I wonder if I could have a few words with you?"

"What aboot?"

"Lady Martin-Macintosh. I've just come from the hospital.
She probably has a fractured hip."

"Aye. Well, she couldnae expect much else. Falling affa chair
at her age. Mind you, I'm sorry to hear it."

The postscript seemed unnatural generosity. Eyes narrowed
against sunlight were fixed on the chocolates. I had been right
about my temptation; at current prices the great British sweet
is becoming a real luxury.

"Was you wanting to come in? The room's no ready. But I
canny help that."

The room seemed ready enough to me, packed with shining
furniture and more flowers in the smallish window, strictly a
showpiece for visitors, rarely used. Mrs. Wilson's marriage tea
set was in a display cabinet and there was a photograph of a man
framed in Woolworth gilt over the mantelpiece, this flanked by
two china dogs and four small vases, the arrangement highly
formal, like the shelf for household gods in a Chinese kitchen.
I put the chocolates on a six-sided table covered with a lace
cloth. The Victoriana all around me would have fetched big
prices in New York, including my rocker, which squeaked every time I moved. The smell of onions was very strong.

"This is a lovely spot up here."

"Aye, no bad. Not easy for the messages, though. The vans
disnae come up. Still, I wouldna mind that if it wusnae for the
holiday folk. Yon woman in that chair! Brazen I calls it. It wusnae like this when we came here."

"You've been here some time?"

"Aye. Six years. Me and Wullie came frae Glasca. Tae retire. This place wusnae much when we got it, but we done it up. Spent oor savings daeing it. Then he was took."

"I'm sorry."

"Aye, I miss him. I never thought I'd end my days going out to the cleaning. Is that what you came aboot? What I saw at the big hoose?"

"Yes."

"Well, I didnae see a thing. Like I told you. The ambulance was awa' when I got off the bus."

"You sometimes helped over at the bungalow, Mrs. Wilson?"

"Aye. Once a week. Right fussy she was, too. Things had to be in their places. Nothing moved. But I'll say this for her, she wusnae mean. Five pounds at Christmas, that's what I got. We got on fine so long as I did just what she wanted, and before I finished she'd have a good look around. To see if I'd moved anything, ye ken? I got a real shock when I saw the place after the accident. Everything higgledy-piggledy. It was my day to do the bungalow, you see. So I went straight over."

"And did you tidy up?"

"I didnae get the chance. Mr. Kennet was there. He said I was to leave everything, his wife would do it. I was to work back at the big hoose the day. Before I could get much of a look, he had me oot on the porch and the door locked. Queerlike thing, that, I must say. As if I'd pinch something just because the old lady wusnae there. Right angry it made me, I can tell you. I thought aboot giving me notice right then."

Indignation made Mrs. Wilson change color. I allowed this to subside before my next question.

"Did you get a chance to see the chair the old lady stood on? Whether it was broken?"

"I couldnae say. I was just inside the door, then oot again. He as good as pushed me. A queer business altogether, I'm thinking. I mean what would the old body be packing up for? And standing on chairs?"

"She was coming to London with me."

"Eh? Mercy! Whatever for? And why would she be needing to pack up things in the hoose for a trip to London?"

"She meant to go on to India afterwards."

"*What?* No that place she was aye talkin' aboot? Where she had a friend or somethin'?"

"Yes."

"And what would Mrs. Kennet be saying to that?"

"She didn't approve."

"And nae wonder! An old body at her age. Still . . ."

There was silence in that front parlor. I felt that Mrs. Wilson had now been given a clear lead to indicate which of the two parties she worked for at Tigh-na-Claddach she favored, but a couple of pounds of chocolates didn't earn this kind of confidence. Her face announced that though she mightn't be a retainer of long standing she had her loyalties, that mouth a tightened clothesline from one plump cheek to the other. I considered putting a five-pound note—the sum mentioned as the height of generosity—on top of the chocolates, but decided the time wasn't ripe. I used a gentle prod.

"Lady Martin-Macintosh used to talk to you about India?"

"Times. She didn't like Arran, that was plain enough. But I never thought she'd go. And what would she be taking that picture for?"

"She was fond of it."

"Aye, I ken that. But what a thing! A lot of folk eating supper, and you canny see them proper. What's that for a picture?"

"Mrs. Wilson, could you say what chair she would be likely to climb on to lift the painting down?"

"Oh, aye. Nae doot aboot that. Yon red thing. It was kept handy by her armchair. She used it as a table. She was awful set on it. Had it made for her, she said."

"And it was a solid chair?"

"It didnae wobble or anything, if that's what you mean. Just what are you getting at, mister?"

Mrs. Wilson was now sitting up very straight, large red hands tucked into each other as though this was the only way she could quieten their lust to be getting on with polishing something. She hadn't been as much use as I had hoped, but it was still necessary to buy her silence. I did this as I stood, sliding a five-pound note over on top of the chocolates.

"Thank you very much for your help, Mrs. Wilson. And I'd be grateful if you'd say nothing about my visit to anyone."

She didn't like the instruction, but liked the money, pretending not to see it as she heaved herself up.

"Well, then," she said, adding quickly, "Is it an operation for the old body?"

"Probably."

"That could see her with the pneumonia. It's the way they go at her age."

I was watched down the path. The mock blonde had been busy. There was now a small table beside the two deck chairs, with a tray on it holding glasses and a pitcher of something that looked like lemonade but had probably been livened up by gin.

"Such a hot day," she said. "A positive miracle in Scotland, isn't it?"

The old man was leaning on his spade having a rest, not seeming to watch, but doing it. Mrs. Wilson was in the porch picking dead flower heads off her plants.

I nodded and smiled.

"Wouldn't you like a drink?"

"Sorry, but I can't wait."

"Stinker," the lady said.

The ex-colonials' club was humming by the time I got to it, five cars and a man on a bench half hidden by hay drinking beer. One of the cars had a nonlocal look, a bright blue Audi coupe, the kind of transport bought by Britons who want to indicate that they have made it, but still consider a Mercedes just slightly obvious advertising. The car had white "GB" lettering on its backside to indicate that its owners dashed down to the French Riviera for the odd long weekend, and between a battered Morris and a very ancient Volks, it looked strayed from the kind of parking places it was used to.

As I got out of the Avenger, the man with the beer stood, shouting across the crop between us.

"Paul Harris?"

"Yes."

"Jeffrey Fanning-Mackie at your service."

He came toward me on a path trampled down earlier through long grass, about six feet tall, brown curly hair with a ginger tinge, trimmed but still luxuriant mustache, the kind of body frame that would make a chain-store drip-dry look like a Hathaway shirt, and with no need for the eye patch. He was wearing a greenish tweed jacket and harmonizing slacks, a cerise shirt open at the neck on sunburn and more hair which said the lot up top wasn't tinted—oldish clothes casually elegant in a way I can never achieve even when I set out expensively to try, which isn't often. When he got close I saw that his eyes had a greenish tinge.

"How the hell did you get here?"

He grinned. Fine teeth, too.

"In my own boat. One of my vices. I even had a boat when I was living in New York. Kept it out on Long Island. In these parts it frees you from all kinds of travel complications. I hear a rumor that there are a couple of five-foot yellow Ming vases hidden out on Mull ever since one of our splendid Scottish soldiers looted the pair from the summer palace in Peking during those Boxer troubles. So I just get in my boat and go, arriving at some crumbling mansion on the motor scooter I carry aboard. Surprise element, you see. Rather throws prospective sellers off balance and I have their treasure all tied up for auction with us before they can even get around to thinking about consulting one of our rivals."

He took out a gold cigarette case and offered it. I shook my head.

"Trying to preserve your life, are you? It's no use. Something else gets you. Probably the booze. Enjoying Arran? Bit trippery, isn't it? We do the thing rather better up my way. Tourists come down our road and we shoot at them. Pretending we were after rabbits. But the word gets around that we're madly eccentric and practically no trespassing is the result. Amazingly peaceful, even in July and August."

"Can I buy you another drink?"

He shook his head. "No, thanks. This beer has much too far to travel in its pipes. You said you couldn't get in anyplace else?"

"That's right."

"I'd have tried harder. Is the food as bad as the décor in there?"

"Yes."

"Then we'll eat on my boat. It's at Lamlash."

"You came here picture-hunting?"

He grinned again. "I wouldn't say that. Just that I had a feeling you might sneak off south without our having had a chance to meet. Which would have been a pity. We need all the Far Eastern contacts we can get. And it was a damn good excuse to go cruising and charge the diesel fuel to expenses. Ready? We'll use your car. I walked from where I left my dinghy."

"I'd like to change my shirt."

He poured out the rest of his beer onto gravel. "Good for the weeds."

I took his glass and went into the bar. All the customers except one were known to me by sight. Seychelles lifted a hand in greeting, but went on talking to his victim for this evening, who had heard it all before too often but was still held transfixed by those Ancient Mariner eyes. Hendy was up at the bar testing out the stranger for his free-drinks potential, both standing facing each other with empty glasses in their hands, which gave me the feeling that the new arrival was putting up quite a resistance. He was smallish, dark, with streaks of gray at the temples, dressed well behind his years in lemon trousers and matching shirt. I liked his bracelet. He had to be the Audi owner. I went up to them.

"How's the Land-Rover?"

Hendy's look would have done justice to deep personal grief.

"Bad news. I've got to get another gearbox. The garage are trying to find a reconditioned one over on the mainland, but even if they manage that it's still going to cost a packet."

The stranger had been looking at me, but when I looked at him he turned away and ordered two more half pints from George, giving Hendy and me the privacy of his back.

"How are you getting about?" I asked.

"Bicycle. It's a helluva nuisance. Makes you realize Arran's all hills. I phoned Tigh-na-Claddach to ask about Lady Martin-Macintosh but I couldn't get an answer. Do you know if she's all right?"

"No. She had a fall. She's in hospital."

He stared. "You mean *another* fall?"

"That's right. Insisted on going back to her cottage. They suspect a broken hip."

"Oh, good Lord! That's terrible. Awful for Mrs. Kennet. She was upset enough last night. Has Angus come home?"

"I saw him this morning when I went up there. Lady Eloise was in bed, fine. But it seems she got up when her daughter wasn't in the cottage."

Hendy looked solemn. "Dizzy spell. I thought the doctor was being far too casual about her last night. She's at a dangerous age."

"I couldn't agree more," I said.

Hendy was obviously keeping the stranger to himself; I wasn't introduced. I put the Honorable Jeffrey's glass on the counter and went up to my room. Emerging from it ten minutes later, I almost bumped into a girl coming out of the door next to mine.

We both stood back from near impact. It was difficult to guess at her age. Green eye shadow was the only color in a dead-white face framed by a twenties straight haircut, black fringe to her eyebrows, then cut evenly all around her head from chin level. She was wearing three strands of bright beads, a pink trouser suit with a heavy white knit cardigan over it, and looked crumpled from long-distance travel. Her voice was southern England still streaked with cockney, which these days meant that she could be anything from an eccentric dancer in a Soho striptease to a senior lecturer in economics at London University.

"Is there a bathroom in the house?"

I told her that you needed a chart to find it.

"All I've found is doors. Unmarked."

"You didn't go far enough. It's down those stairs to the landing, up the other ones to the dark passage, and then four along on your right."

"I didn't much like the look of that passage. Tell me, have you a light in your room?"

"Yes, two."

"We've got three sockets with nothing in them."

"Just a slight administrative oversight. George will fix you up. He's barman just now. You'll have him as waiter later."

"From which I take it you're eating out?"

"Yes."

"Is there a decent restaurant on the island?"

"I haven't found one. A friend is feeding me."

"You've been staying here for a while?"

"Several days."

She smiled. This didn't affect her eyes at all, but it did lighten up her face.

"Nice to know that guests survive."

I went with her down to the landing and from there indicated the route up into gloom, waiting to see if she got the right door.

The opening of this spotlighted her and she stood for a moment looking back down toward the landing as though wanting to be quite sure she would know me again when we next met. It was an appraisal devoid of any sex interest, and I wasn't flattered.

EIGHT

Jeffrey's boat was a thirty-five-foot welded steel job topped off by a lofty bridge all glassed in and with a couple of anchored fishing chairs aft for serious sport, the rest of the fittings for play, and expensive. When he admitted to having had it shipped over from the States on the well deck of a freighter, I decided that being an auctioneer's provincial agent is a great trade for our time, or his wife had money; probably both. He was a perfect host, the bar adequate for a two-week cruise and the fridge deep-freeze compartment packed with Angus fillets, two of which he proposed to fry for us later.

After I had admired everything without envy—it wasn't my kind of boat—we took our drinks to the stern cockpit, sitting in the fishing chairs to look at the town of Lamlash from the water. In evening sunlight it was prettier than ever, a delightful village in which to wait pleasantly for death. Every now and then I lifted binoculars to spy on someone working in a garden featuring palm trees, or people out on terraces with glasses in their hands doing what we were doing. Stillness and lingering warmth made it impossible to believe that we were above latitude fifty, parallel to Labrador.

Jeffrey was a more relaxing companion than the major. He

hadn't the slightest desire to serve me large portions of his past life, and I returned the compliment, the silence almost total until he brought up the second round of large whiskies.

"Bliss, isn't it?" he said, handing me a glass.

"Yes."

"Getting a weakness for Scotland?"

"I've always had it. But come the rains and I want out of here fast."

"The rain is why we're so green."

"Malaysia's green. It rains for twenty-five minutes every day, usually all at once. That's a good arrangement."

"You Eastern-born are all schizophrenic about place."

I looked at him. "You've come home, have you?"

"I think so. My wife isn't sure. She liked the States. Even the hazards of Manhattan. Have you had another look at the alleged Renoir recently?"

"The owner's had an accident. Her house is shut up."

"Oh. Serious?"

"It's probably a broken hip. And I make her at least seventy-five."

He appeared to be waiting for me to say more, but I didn't.

"So if I just rolled up there and told them I'd heard they had a Renoir someplace, you don't think I'd be warmly received?"

"From what I've seen, people don't call casually at Tigh-na-Claddach too much. They have a big dog called Rufus."

Jeff wasn't looking as disappointed as I had expected. I asked a question that had been on my mind.

"The old girl claims her picture ought to be worth about a quarter of a million. What would you say to that, if it *is* a Renoir?"

"What sort of size?"

"About three feet by three."

"The lead-in to 'La Galette' you told me about might create special interest. But quarter of a million, never. Fifty thousand, maybe. More likely forty, even thirty-five."

"That could be a nasty shock to the family."

"It's still a nice round sum."

I sat there wondering if I would rate being shot at for thirty-five thousand. The answer was probably yes. I asked another question.

"If you had stolen a Renoir and couldn't sell it in this country, where would you take it?"

"Rome. That's the new in place for any crook deal in the art line. You book a suite in a good hotel and put out feelers. Before long you're contacted by a buyer for a multimillionaire who has lost faith in the stock market, Swiss banks, and even gold, but still sees a long-term future in established Impressionists. Especially small Impressionists which can be kept on board the big yacht in which he is evading everybody's taxes."

"Did Hodson take his loot to Rome?"

"That's a leading question I'm not answering."

"But you've heard more about him?"

"A little. Enough. And in strict confidence. So stop digging."

"Supposing I got you in to see the picture somehow, how good would your guess be that the old lady is right?"

"My reaction would be more instinct than training."

"You get some kind of psychic waves from the object?"

"It sounds mad, but yes. About six months ago I came on an Awaji vase. In Brechin, of all places."

"What the hell's an Awaji vase?"

"I'd never heard of them either. The glaze wasn't all that good and the coloring not too exciting, but something said: This is interesting. It was. From a private kiln on a Japanese island. Four hundred years old. Sold for just under six thousand to Tokyo interests. They're buying back like mad all their national treasures that somehow got shipped to Europe last century while they weren't watching. I knew this, of course, but I was still astonished. Nothing like as astonished as the owner. His wife said she'd liked it for roses."

Jeff knew how to grill a steak, crisp outside, red in the middle.

He had brought along one of his bargain wines, which I sipped slowly and with real pleasure. We didn't eat until nearly ten and afterward he rowed me ashore in the dinghy, a stout black rubber job which he could just deflate and stow in a locker.

I sat in the Avenger watching him row out again toward a cruiser blazing with lights that were draining his battery reserves, then turned the car and drove along under Lamlash street lighting to the turnoff leading to my hotel. About a hundred yards up this I parked for ten minutes, turned the car again, and drove back through Lamlash, using only my side lights. There was no sign of Jeff on the stern deck of his boat, but the cabin portholes and two transom windows glowed.

The high fencing at Tigh-na-Claddach must really have been put up only to keep out deer. It was supported out onto rocks by iron poles set in concrete, but these stopped where the going got too rough to be suitable for hoofs and even at half tide I was able to get around the end without wetting my feet. I paused for a moment or two to see if there was any reaction from a guard dog, then eased along behind the bungalow to a corner which gave me a view of the big house. There was still light enough for a dedicated gardener to be at work, but no sign at all of Anne among the rose beds. What I didn't like was the open French window in the Tigh-na-Claddach sitting room and, just audible, the booming of a television sound track.

The back door to the bungalow was locked, but its upper half had an inset of six small panes. I wrapped a handkerchief around the head of my flashlight and took out the lower-right-hand square of glass, most of the tinkling from this being contained by the kitchenette beyond. My groping hand had to deal with a bolt as well as the knob of the Yale.

I went into Eloise's house by the rear entrance like a member of the criminal classes with a possible six-month sentence to hard labor ahead, but buoyed up by a basic purpose that was moderately moral. I could see well enough to keep from bumping into the stove or the refrigerator, and though the sitting room was veranda-darkened, I didn't use the flash in there either, conscious of those French windows across a lawn. Once again I was aware of how very much Eloise had been under observation here, her lights-out time subject to check, even movement from room to room visible to a watcher using those binoculars, about as private in this place as a nesting bird of rare species under the constant curiosity of ornithologists.

Mrs. Wilson hadn't been allowed to tidy up, but someone had done the job. The room was about as I remembered it, a closely packed clutter of small tables and whatnots looking as though they had never been disturbed by an old lady crashing down among them. I made out the kris again suspended from its cords but on the white fireplace wall, kept bare to honor a painting, there was no painting, just a lighter patch where it had hung.

I hadn't risked jail to look at pictures and didn't waste time speculating as to what had happened to a maybe Renoir. The chair that Eloise used as a table was where Mrs. Wilson had said it ought to be, flanking the fireplace. With light fading fast, my inspection had to be mostly by feel, but fingers told me a lot: Yokohama red lacquer work, circa 1935, every bit of its back and legs covered in writhing carved dragons. There had been a great vogue for these at one time and they were mass-produced, mainly for front halls. Here they served the useful function of discouraging anyone invited to sit on one from staying very long. My parents' house in Singapore had four of the things in the entrance area and when the wrong people tried to gate-crash our stately home they got a polite, but slippery, welcome on a highly waxed seat area while the houseboy flip-flopped off to find out that the mistress was not at home. As a child I was sometimes set up on one of them to have shoes changed and I can remember a small bottom going into perilous skids.

I remembered something else about those chairs: they were made in two pieces to facilitate export packing, a solid slab of back and rear legs from which the seat portion and front legs could be detached, the two sections sealed together by pegs which drove through the slabs to a pair of lacquered screw-on caps at the back. Being wooden, the caps loosened easily and my brother invented the delightful game of just slightly unscrewing all eight of them in our hall, so that the chairs looked all right, but when sat on there was a sharp crack and a fanged dragon came forward with the loosened back to have a bite at the victim's neck.

I once got beaten with the back of a hairbrush when caught in the act of exploiting my brother's discovery, which made an immediate check of those back caps the natural thing for me to do now. The ones on Eloise's chair were so tight I couldn't budge them.

There was just enough light in the room still for me to reconstruct the set for an accident. Eloise would certainly have used this chair to get down her picture. If there was a stepladder in the bungalow she couldn't carry it about, but it would be easy enough for her to tow the chair out from its usual place and set it in front of the fireplace, as I was doing. The projecting brick hearth kept the back legs from getting any wall support, which meant that when Eloise had stood on the chair, leaning forward to get hold of the picture, her weight must have been thrust against the rear slab. I put a knee on the seat and pushed at the back. There was a crack. The chair had started to separate into two pieces, and only a slight tug was needed to finish the job.

I propped the rear slab up against the mantel, checking the screw caps around at the back. These were still firm. The pegs sticking out of the seat portion felt much shorter than they should have been to drive through to those caps, and they were covered with something sticky. I shrouded my torch in a handkerchief and switched it on. The tacky substance was a plastic wood adhesive which would have set hard in a matter of hours, the chair then as solid as it had ever been. The pegs hadn't been sawn off, but broken with a hammer, which was a neat touch, for if by any outside chance the chair was dismantled during a police check and the severed pegs discovered, there would still be nothing to suggest that the breaks had been made deliberately, and a repair job might have been done months ago. You can't date a glue which has set.

I lowered the front portion of the chair to the rug, switched out the torch and put it down on the hearth, then stood, staring at a still visible whiter patch on a white wall, thinking about phoning the police from here now. If I did, round one was going to see all the focus on a breaking and entry by me, a situation from which it wouldn't be too easy to talk myself into the clear.

There was a slight scraping sound. I swung around as the room lights came on. The man I had been thinking about was standing inside the door from the porch. He didn't have a rifle, just the stout knobkerrie he took on his evening walk around the grounds with Rufus. He threw this, not a bad aim for an impulse shot. It missed me but got a cloisonné vase on the mantelshelf. The stick clattered onto bricks.

Angus didn't rush me. I'd have preferred him berserk. He came almost slowly, clearing a path for himself, a sofa sent spinning on ball casters, a small table kicked over. What he was feeling was under control, and this was formidable. His arms were thrust out but his hands weren't fists; the fingers were flat together for chop blows. I tried the old trick of arms up, left extended, right back for a Queensberry rules defensive punch. To my surprise he fell for it, lunging as I kicked up with my right foot in what wasn't quite the snake strike. He saw his mistake in time to twist to take that blow on a thigh, then swung his body back to close, chopping fast twice for my neck. I did two body jerks, getting those blows on collarbones, real thumps. I could see this bastard training for infighting with blocks of wood, that fetish. He was in good shape from a lot more than golf exercise, ready for mixed tactics if I was playing it that way, his punch straight for my stomach, but with a fractional delay which let me take a space-softened blow just above one hip. This time he didn't see the kick up with my left leg. My foot landed where I had intended, in the groin, not full force, but enough to send him staggering back, almost losing balance against one end of the sofa. He recovered faster than I thought he would, moving in again, no more karate, his hands claws. It wasn't easy to let him go for my throat, but I did, steel clamps on my neck. I was just able to get a thumb into the corner of his right eye, pressing on the ball.

He screamed and reeled back. I stood snorting air into my lungs, and had to let him reel too far. Before I realized the next round was to be with weapons, he had spun about to yank the kris down from its cords. The only thing within my reach was a bronze incense burner. I threw that. In dodging he went off balance. I bent to grab one carved lacquer leg, lifting half a chair.

I had a shield and he took his time. The blade of the chopper had been kept bright with metal polish. His advance was splay-footed, like a Japanese sumo wrestler's. I saw his eyes, calculating, still not maddened by a kill lust. This was business. Fear was a big chill in my stomach.

The blade came down. Half a chair met it. The kris sliced through smooth lacquer and the solid carving beneath it with a noise like an old rafter collapsing. There was a thump on the floor. I swayed from impact shock, holding not much more than one leg, a torchbearer suffering from fatigue staggers. Angus smiled.

The kris went up again. I thought the growl was from his throat, but it wasn't. The dog's leap was probably directed at me, but off direction. Two hundred pounds of Rufus smacked into Angus from behind. He went down, and I heard the thud as his head hit a protruding fragment of red-lacquered dragon. The kris was at my feet. Angus lay still. The dog was sprawled beside him, looking dazed, and then slowly it got up, hindquarters first, like a camel.

"Get out!" I shouted.

For a moment the brute watched me aiming a chair leg, then

he went fast. I didn't score a hit, but there was a clattering from the veranda, followed by a howling out on the lawn.

I stood listening to the alarm klaxon of my heart. Angus's blood, not so bright as sliced red lacquer up against one side of his head, was beginning to put a stain on a gold Kashan rug. Fighting nausea, I went down on my knees, pushing at a body, rolling it over. The gash went from above the hairline well down onto his forehead. It looked like the life was flowing out of him from it, though his heart still pumped away, if a lot quieter than mine. He began to breathe like a man going under from an ether pad.

It was a moment for clear thinking, but I didn't manage it, driven by a half-formed idea that I had to get him onto a bed. I stood, then hauled him by the armpits toward Eloise's bedroom, dropping him to switch on lights. There were two suitcases with their lids open on the bed and I had to lift these down. Levering him up took time. He was still making that wheezing noise and I couldn't seem to get my own breathing right. At one stage he was face downward on a white coverlet that was going to cause a panic when it reached the laundry, then I got him over on his back again.

There was a washbasin in the room but no towels and I had to go to the bathroom for these, coming back with an armful, wringing them out in cold water for compresses that went pink almost at once. I remembered ice and in the kitchenette stood stabbing cubes out of two trays, thinking about what it could mean to me if Angus died. I ought to phone the doctor, then run for it.

On the way back with cubes in a bowl, I put out the sitting room lights. The bedroom window looked out on wire and empty moor. I shut the door and then made toweling bags with the ice, covering his whole head with these except his nose and mouth. He was breathing now like a man who might start choking at any minute, almost a snore. Diluted blood had soaked his shirt and matted the lapels of his tweed jacket.

I heard the door open. Against a square of blackness Jeffrey Fanning-Mackie was standing to watch me.

We hadn't talked much. I was glad of his takeover. I held the roll of adhesive tape from Eloise's medicine box while Jeff cut the size he wanted. He had already used scissors to take off a good deal of Angus's front hair.

"Get that towel away," he said.

The blood had coagulated. Jeff sponged carefully around the edges of the wound, very professional. I didn't ask where he had learned his first aid. I didn't ask any questions, not wanting him to start on me.

"Unless he gets stitches in this, he's going to have a real scar," Jeff said.

"It's blood loss that worries me."

"About two donations of plasma worth."

"There's a trail back into the next room."

"Even then. He'll feel a bit low for a while. And have a very sore head. That's all."

"No need for a doctor?"

"You want to call one?"

"No."

"I didn't think you would." He looked at me. "If the old lady has any medicinal brandy you'd better have a shot."

"I'm all right."

He put on the tape neatly, one quick movement, then a delicate tapping down of the edges. He might have been night surgeon in a casualty ward. He went to the washbasin and turned on the tap. It was the moment for questioning to start, but he didn't say anything.

Angus's breathing had changed again. He was now sounding like a man having a slightly bad dream, but not bad enough to bring on a heart attack. Jeff picked up one of the bloodied towels and started to use it to dry his hands, moving out of the way to let me in to the washbasin. I didn't see him cross the room, but he was on the other side of it when he said:

"What's all the luggage for?"

He was standing by a trunk open under the window, which I hadn't even noticed. He bent down and pulled up a fur stole that would be useful for chilly nights in Ooty during the monsoon.

"The old lady was planning to travel?"

"Yes."

"Where?"

"India."

"You were going with her?"

That was smart deduction.

"Only to London."

"As escort for the painting?"

"Yes."

"You still think it's a Renoir?"

"I just wouldn't know. Whatever it is, it should be hanging next door. But it isn't."

If the news disappointed him, this didn't show. He came back to the other side of the bed and stood looking down at the patient, a doctor making his rounds of the surgical ward in which he expects to find no postoperative complications, thanks to his skill.

"Couldn't the picture be up at the big house for safekeeping?" he asked.

"I mean to find out. Did you come here by the drive? Were there any lights up there?"

"I always use main entrances. There were no lights."

"How about a Mini?"

"No sign of one. It could be round the back."

"It's always left out front. Anne can't be home."

"What a lot you know about the owner's habits around here. I was wondering when you were going to mention Mrs. Kennet. Shouldn't she be told about her husband?"

"How can I do that if I don't know where she is?"

"Meantime you search her house?"

"Yes."

"Another breaking and entry?"

I stared at him. "So you had a good look around this bungalow before you joined me?"

"Smashing a pane seems a rather unsubtle way of getting in."

"I'm observant, like you say. Last time I was here I saw that all the windows had burglar catches. The back door was the only weak spot. But we shouldn't have any trouble getting in the big house."

He smiled, but it wasn't standard issue of the Fanning-Mackie charm. "To what extent am I expected to be an accessory in all this?"

"That's up to you, isn't it? You can get on your scooter and go back to your boat anytime you like. And thanks for the medical assistance."

"You needed it."

"All right, I needed it. Can we leave this man now?"

"Oh, yes. He'll wake up feeling he's being punished for his sins. Whatever they may be. You don't want to tidy up around here?"

"We'll leave that to his wife."

Jeff shrugged and moved toward the door to the sitting room, opening it. We left Angus snorting in the dark and groped our way across to the porch. I meant to leave without any advertising that the bungalow had been in use. It was quite a shock when Jeff switched on the sitting room lights and stood looking over a battlefield.

"Fascinating for the police," he said.

My first reactions to this man's personality were undergoing some sharp revisions. When we were down on soft grass he said:

"Pity about the picture being missing. I was counting on having a look at it."

"I'm sure. But not to the point of breaking and entering?"

It was a good half minute before he spoke again. "If it is a

Renoir, what do you get out of all this activity on behalf of Lady Martin-Macintosh?"

"Nothing."

It was too dark to see his face, but I was quite certain it registered disbelief. I decided to move to the attack.

"You've been in London since we talked on the phone. A quick trip to consult with your directors. They sent you haring back up here to see whether I might turn out to be a lead to Hodson. Or maybe Hodson himself pretending to be a Singapore businessman."

"No. My directors knew who you were, all right. They'd been put onto some cousin of yours who works in the City. Know the man I mean?"

"I ought to. He was my major charity for years, as my so-called London agent. I finally had to sack him for incompetence."

"That may well account for some of the things he said about you."

We went up onto the small terrace outside the sitting room, where a long window was invitingly open. I didn't look to see whether Jeff was following me. A faint glow from logs guided me to switches by the door to the hall. Lights showed that Jeff was continuing to be an accessory after the act; he was inside the room, with the French window now closed, looking around it, his expression saying that poverty is no excuse for bad taste.

Angus had been drinking alone by the TV waiting until the end of the late-night movie before going out to walk his dog, a single empty glass on a table by the armchair opposite the set. There were unused glasses on the whisky tray and I was pretty certain that if Anne had been here, sharing any part of her husband's evening, she would have been at the whisky, too, the evidence another used glass.

I poured myself a double. Jeff, an expert on log fires, crossed to this one, picking up the bellows and getting to work with trained skill. I left him and went upstairs.

Anne and Angus had separate bedrooms, hers neat, everything put away, with no painting under the bed. His was like a theatrical dressing room, a single, dormitory-type bed surrounded by clutter, on the walls and flat surfaces his trophies from living, most of these, except for three golf cups, remembering the schoolboy, which had obviously been his only successful period. There were pictures of Angus the boxer, and in cricket whites, and one of three rows in a rugger team, all of the youths sitting or standing with thumbs behind their biceps to exaggerate muscle development. I looked around for a picture of Anne, but there wasn't one; no reminders of the Orient either, except for a silk dressing gown flung over a chair, which was flamboyant with embroidered peonies. The place was no setting for a Renoir, even one packaged for transit, and I didn't think I would find the Kennets' hope of a fortune stashed away in a coal cellar, or an outhouse, or Angus's workshop, so sped up the rest of my search. The other bedrooms upstairs were scarcely furnished and easy to check, and the room Eloise had used below revealed nothing either. There was a dog's bed in the cloakroom near the front door, but no dog in it.

Rufus was by a revived fire, already accepting a stranger as the right kind of man for him. Jeff sat in a chair with sunken springs, a whisky in one hand, the other out over the arm, just touching the mastiff's head. Rufus started to get up when he saw me.

"Sit," Jeff said, with quiet authority. "This beast was clawing at the window. He's had some kind of shock. Came in almost on his belly."

"He's failed as a watchdog and knows it. Too much inbreeding."

Jeff looked at his watch. "Twenty past one. I've been wondering about Mrs. Kennet. What if she comes back?"

"We offer her a whisky and get her to tell us where she's been." I stood staring down at Jeff. "Your man Hodson put the Kennets wise to the fact that Mum had a Renoir."

Jeff didn't say anything.

"On that trip to London you were put fully into the picture about Hodson. Why was he sacked from Harwell-Speed?"

"He wasn't sacked. He resigned. There is no evidence that he did anything."

"All right. What do your directors *think* he did?"

"Why should I tell you?"

"I'm offering you a deal. Put me in your picture, I'll put you in mine. But on one condition—you don't go to the police with anything I tell you."

He looked at the fire, not caring for any deals he hadn't arranged himself. It was some time before he said:

"I suppose that's fair enough."

"Then you start."

Rufus sighed and stretched out. He was certainly not the kind of dog who would die from a broken heart because of an owner switch. Jeff took his time to choose the facts to serve me, like a man forking over a green salad in which he suspects there may be a caterpillar. When he did speak, every word was gift-wrapped with reluctance.

"It is just possible that Hodson smuggled three pictures worth about a hundred thousand each to the Continent. Sold them privately in Geneva and banked the money there for his clients. Less his commission."

I was very interested. "The idea being his clients avoid paying a thirty percent capital gains tax on a sale in this country?"

"Yes."

"What about insurance on those pictures?"

"There wasn't any."

"How come?"

"It could be that Hodson discovered them."

"Wait a minute. How do you know those supposed clients of his had those pictures if there was no insurance record? Or any other record?"

"We don't know, that's the point. Only suspect. The deceased owners of the estate had been pretty eccentric. Descended from a long line of magpies. A complete Sèvres dinner service was found in the attic. We sold that for the heirs, along with a lot of other things, to help pay death duties."

"Surely the tax people insisted on an inventory and valuation of everything in the house?"

"Yes, but we weren't the official valuers."

"Are you saying that Hodson got there before the official valuers?"

"That was perfectly in order. We were working for the family. The tax people had their own valuers. It is just possible that Hodson didn't give us a complete report on everything he found in the house."

"What makes you suspect that?"

"Well, a chatty daily help gave us a description of three pictures she had seen several times in a storeroom. These had disappeared before the official valuers took over. And a month or two later three pictures that were sold very privately in Switzerland sounded remarkably like the missing paintings described by the cleaning woman."

The private espionage network run by the big boys in the fine-art selling business could probably give some useful tips to the CIA or British Intelligence.

"Distinguished family, are they?" I asked. "The people who saved themselves about a hundred thousand by using Hodson?"

"I wouldn't say distinguished; no."

"Just a quiet county lot living in a big house who had become terribly worried about what death duties and inflation were doing to their standard of living?"

Jeff sipped his whisky, then said, "It's your turn now."

"After I had met Lady Eloise and been asked to help sell her picture, I was asked on a day's fishing by a Major Henderson-Pratt, who lives here. He and Angus play golf together. Up in the hills I was shot at three times from a rifle with a telescopic sight."

If Jeff was sharply interested, he concealed this very well.

"You think the gunman was Kennet?"

"Yes."

"What kind of a target were you?"

"Near perfect."

"He must be a bad shot."

"He meant to miss. I was being warned to take my curiosity away from Arran."

"Where was the major when this happened?"

"About half a mile away. Out in a dinghy on water."

"He must have heard the shots."

"We'd been hearing shots all afternoon. From a keeper after rabbits, the major said."

"You didn't tell him you'd been shot at?"

"No."

"Because you suspect collusion between him and Kennet?"

"It's a possibility."

Jeff stared at me. "When I was crossing that sitting room in the dark, my foot touched something. Damn sharp blade. Nearly cut my fingers. Was Kennet using that?"

"Yes."

"So tonight he meant to kill you?"

"Yes."

"Because you'd found something that incriminated him with regard to an accident to the old lady?"

"I was trying to reconstruct that accident when he switched on the lights."

"That's not good enough, Paul. What had you found?"

"He'd fixed a chair so it would collapse under her."

"And you're not going to the police about this?"

"Not yet."

"That still makes me an accessory in your cover-up from the law."

"It may only be for a matter of hours. And I have your promise."

He gave me a cold smile. "There's a matter of principle involved."

"Sure. And at the moment I haven't got evidence against Kennet that would stand up in court. The chair is just not enough."

"Your breaking and entry is also a consideration?"

"All right, it is."

Jeff put his glass down on the bricks of the hearth. He sat back again, looking at me.

"At what point did you really become involved in all this?"

"When I was shot at. Being a target for bullets always involves me. Even when the gunman is firing to miss. There was also the fact that I didn't think an old lady was safe in her house. I was going to get her away. Whether or not the picture was a Renoir didn't seem too important."

Jeff closed his eyes, as though suddenly sleepy.

"It looks as though you arrived at an awkward time for the Kennets."

"Yes. They have something on the boil with your man Hodson."

Jeff looked at me again. "He is *not* our man! Tell me, what would Lady Martin-Macintosh's reaction be if she discovered that the Kennets had been planning to steal her picture and sell it?"

"She'd hound them into the ground without mercy. Even if it took her last breath to do it."

"Her daughter?"

"She's adopted."

"I see. What's Mrs. Kennet like?"

"The first time we met, I knew that she and I could make a good life together."

He stared at me in total disbelief. A rogue feeling of this kind, quite unconditioned by reason or sensible prudence, was utterly beyond his understanding. I was certain that the Honorable Mrs. Fanning-Mackie's pedigrees had been carefully inspected before marriage had even been contemplated. Probably the checkup had been just as careful from her side. The British upper classes still do a lot more of this research before matrimony than they would care to admit, the emphasis being on family money first, healthy blood stock second. If you have the money, health doesn't matter so much.

Rufus was now snoring. Jeff, embarrassed for the first time since our meeting, avoided looking at me, putting out a shoe to touch the dog's flank, just as he might have done at home. Then, when silence had lasted too long, he made an effort.

"What's the next move?"

"The next move takes me back to my hotel and bed. I need sleep. If you'd like a lift to Lamlash, I think we could pack your scooter in the back of my car."

He stood up.

"No, thanks. I'll stick to my own transport."

He seemed reluctant to leave Rufus all alone in a big empty house. I didn't mind doing that. When we reached his scooter, tucked into some bushes near the gate, I said:

"If you're thinking of spending the rest of the night looking for Anne Kennet, she's a tall blonde driving a green Mini."

In the drive to the hotel I put on full heads, the beams splashing over an Audi still parked near the steps to the bar. The front door was unlocked but no lights had been left on and I had to use switches on the way up, forty-candlepower bulbs hanging naked from distant ceilings to produce successive small oases in the gloom. All the windows in my room were shut, the place stuffy, and I lifted a swollen, protesting sash, only able to get it up a few inches. Even with ventilation it was going to be a warm night under layers of blankets, but I was suddenly too tired even to think about peeling these off, instead doing without the flannel pajamas which are the first thing I buy on landing in Britain during the summer, needing them most nights. I climbed into the bed with plenty to think about, but my brain said it had had enough, and closed down.

I woke to a sound that made no sense, a kind of whimpering and very close. Then there were words.

"Tuan, makan berkuah ayer mata."

It was a dream and I didn't move. I heard the same Malay words again, louder this time: "I eat with tears for sauce."

A hand touched my rib cage.

"Tuan, tuan! Take me Singapore. Here I die. Take me Singapore!"

"Aishah!"

Her hands were on my shoulders, then at my neck. Her body slid over onto mine.

"Tuan . . ."

Her hands traveled down, not too fast, but fast enough, the murmuring now wordless, a little sung chorus to the action. The action was within seconds of becoming what she wanted when a door crashed back against a wall. Light from the hall reached the bed. Even in a large room the bang of a handgun was very loud.

NINE

I don't know where that first bullet went, just that I got out of a threatened area fast. Aishah was even faster, the pale glow from a central light exposing a dusky rump disappearing under the bed frame. For some idiot reason I didn't take cover, just stood there, considerably more of an invitation than the dummy at the end of a police college shooting gallery. I had a very strong feeling that if I moved at all now, even for a towel within arm's reach, George's attention would switch to me. As it was, I mightn't have existed. The gun was held out by a man who had been trained to use it, his eyes focused down on the bed. He knew she was underneath it.

It was unnerving that he didn't look or sound in the least like a husband on the brink of a *crime passionel.* There had been no shouting, not even one word; he stood looking positively composed, his hand steady, his normally surly reddish face now completely expressionless. He just meant to do tonight what he had thought about doing for a long time. He fired again, this time aiming for the center of the mattress.

Aishah screamed. It was a long, sharp, piercing note followed by a cadenza of wails, then sobbing, none of this from pain. She hadn't been hit yet, but for all the width of that bed there was enough light in the room for George to make out her shape under it. He still stood upright, almost at attention against the door. Then he began to bend down, but slowly, as though earlier resolution had been invaded by a stab of sentiment. I could literally see him shake this off, then carry on to a crouch.

He could easily have killed me as I came around the foot of the bed, but a total concentration on Aishah blunted his reaction. He raised the gun quickly enough, but too high, the bullet shattering an upper pane of the window. As I hit out at his wrist, the muzzle of a Colt stared in my face for seconds. Then the gun clattered to the floor.

He jerked up as I grabbed the top of his pajama jacket. I could feel the strength in his body, but there was a weird lack of resistance, as though he still couldn't accept my intrusion. Aishah was screaming again. The sound she made bounced back in on us from the lofty echo chamber of the hall. That screeching distracted me. I don't know whether it did him, but he was suddenly fighting back, struggling against my bid to get him flat on a wall. Instead we went down on the floor together, heavily, George on top, splaying his body over mine to hold me.

We were still threshing about when the screaming stopped. Both of us realized at almost the same time that Aishah had escaped and was on the stairs. George flung himself away from me, using the bed to get on his feet. I caught one leg as he made for the door, bringing him down again. This time I was the one who got up. He just lay there, head twisted on his neck, peering out into the hall.

"She's got the gun," I said.

He sat up. He couldn't have been spent physically, but he looked like a man out for the count against the ropes. We heard a door slam at a distance, solid mahogany like most of the doors in this building, then the only sound was the two of us breathing. George pulled himself up by a doorknob. He didn't look at me, going straight out into the hall and across that broad upper landing at not much more than an invalid's pace. I found my dressing gown, put it on, and by the time I was at the railing above the stairs he was halfway down them, bare feet making a flapping noise on each tread, like a man walking in flippers. I watched him cross the halfway landing and go up the flight into the dark corridor. Aishah must have locked herself into the bathroom. There was the noise of fists battering on panels, but it didn't go on for long; then there was weeping, a man's. George was spent. Aishah was safe enough, with or without that gun. I went back into my room and shut the door against a miserable keening.

I sat on the bed, exhausted. It had been quite a night. My part in what had just happened was really a total irrelevance, but this wasn't going to help me to just wipe an incident from my mind. The hopeless human situation has a die stamp that doesn't fade quickly. What Aishah needed was simple enough: back to her own place and her old trade in it. What a time-worn ex-sergeant needed he wasn't likely to get: some core of permanence in a transient's life. I had known a good few like George in the East, all of them by-products of surviving colonialism, Army NCOs turned policemen with the job of trying to keep a nineteenth-century society still functioning. It was often dirty work, well enough paid, but the men doing it only really existed inside their uniforms. Out of these they became shadows in a world that chose not to see them, and off-duty recreation was the charity club or the dance hall. Loneliness had found Aishah for George, together with an illusion of love.

There was now a wind blowing against the house, funneling in on me from a shattered window. The tiredness I felt wasn't the kind that fetches sleep. I began to dress, not really knowing why, and was pulling on trousers when I remembered about the new hotel guests next door. I hadn't seen the girl and the man in lemon trousers together, but they must have come as a pair, in that Audi. It was incredible that they could have slept through gunfire and Aishah's screams, but they had certainly stayed strictly neutral. It could be that they were cowering down under a quilt listening to wild goings-on in a savage north-ern land, though the girl hadn't seemed the cowering type.

Pulling on a sweater, I went out into the hall. I knocked twice, not very loud in case George heard. There was no audible answer. I went into a room still retaining the day's heat from closed windows and a deep silence in which there didn't seem to be any breathing. Light from the hall showed a woman's coat draped over a chair. I went very quietly to the window. The Audi was down in the drive.

It was twenty past three. The bed offered two undented pillows and a smooth coverlet folded back. If there was any night life in Lamlash to which guests from this hotel could just walk, I had certainly missed the advertising for it. The newcomers might have friends on the island, but it seemed improbable, somehow, that the local residents gave the kind of parties which went on until this hour in the morning.

I switched on lights. George had put low-powered bulbs in three sockets, one central, another over the dressing table, a third near enough the bed for reading if you didn't mind risking acute eyestrain. From the look of things in the room it didn't seem the couple from the Audi were too sure about staying on here. Very few things had been taken out of suitcases; there were not even makeup bottles under the mirror. A closet was empty; so were drawers. Three suitcases were tucked in neatly beside a chest of drawers and I lifted them. Two were heavy and one, the largest, almost square, was light, which was curi-ous. What was even more curious, the full suitcases weren't locked, the empty one was.

I went back to my own room for a nail file, then returned to round out a night of illegal activity by putting the light case on top of the chest and getting to work on it with the file. What I did to a resisting lock left very obvious traces on a sprayed gold finish, brute force being necessary before there was a crack and I could lift the lid.

The case had unusual fittings, a thickly padded stop at each corner of the bottom section, with similar pads glued into the lid. I didn't know the exact dimensions of Eloise's painting, but whoever had ordered this convenient carrier to be made certainly did. With the lid lowered, a stolen painting, still in its frame, would be held firmly but without the hard pressure that might damage gilded gesso work.

I couldn't disguise the traces of lock-breaking, but it would be foolish to leave fingerprints, so I got to work with a handkerchief, wondering as I polished about the length of time it was taking the Tigh-na-Claddach painting to reach this carrier. Something, not really a noise, made me look toward a door I had closed.

It was now open. A small gun held very high almost made a third eye staring at me. The other two eyes belonged to the girl with the dark fringe low on her forehead. She had changed from that earlier bright outfit into a dark two-piece for night work, apparently packing the pink away at the same time. The beads had gone, too. Suspended on straps from a left wrist tucked in against her body was one of those small sack-type handbags, this also black. She now looked like the kind of secretary who could always be relied on to cover up for her boss, efficiency what she was selling.

"This may not seem much of a gun, Mr. Harris. I need something small I can wear next to the skin through customs. It's accurate. I check that periodically."

"Shooting at a can in the back garden?"

"I use a palm tree in my courtyard. Wasn't it rather a mistake to put on all these lights for your work?"

"I see that now. Where's your husband?"

"I don't go in for husbands."

"In that case, where's Hodson?"

She said nothing.

"You moved into this hotel because I was here?"

"I can't think of any other reason for moving into this hotel. Pat your pockets."

150

"I don't carry a gun."

"*Pat* them!"

I patted them. "Only car keys and loose change."

"Then shall we go?"

"I'm being taken someplace?"

"You are."

"It's my guess that Hodson prefers just to side-step the law, not break it. Think your colleague will approve of this move?"

"My colleagues do what I tell them."

It is always useful to know who's boss.

"Kidnapping me at the end of a gun could run you both smack up against British justice."

"I can afford a good lawyer."

She smiled. She had those teeth with slight gaps between them that can last a lifetime if you apply fluoride three times a day, a dental ideal, but they somehow make their owner's smile different from other smiles, almost identifying a separate species.

She pulled the door wide and stepped back from it, the gun still held close to her body, its snout signaling. Our progress downstairs was marked by lights switched off, the girl as careful as if she owned the place and the last electricity bill had been a shock. There wasn't a sound from either Aishah or George, both probably slumped into a half-stunned reaction from acute trauma. All I heard was my escort's soft tread on carpet strips as she kept the right range for putting a bullet through the back of my skull if this became necessary. Even in the lower hall and at the opening of the outer door she never moved in close to me; always that careful distance. I had to stand silhouetted against the beginnings of dawn while she reached for the last switch. We went out, leaving a darkened building.

I was to drive the Avenger. A rising wind was lashing treetops as we got into the car, with me obliged to slide over behind the wheel from the passenger seat, never for a moment out of range of that gun. I took the drive at some speed, hitting the deeper

151

potholes, but the bouncing didn't dislodge the steel prodding my pelvis. A woman using a gun as a persuader makes me especially uneasy. She knows, even if adept at kung fu, that she is physically at a disadvantage, so there is always that impulse to pull the trigger just a little bit sooner than a man would. You have to allow for this. I was doing it.

"Left at the gates."

We were going through Lamlash, which didn't brighten my prospects. Even if I managed to crash the car against the steps of the local police station I would be dead and the girl gone long before anyone was out of bed to investigate an accident. There was nothing to connect her with me; no one knew that we had exchanged a few politenesses in a hotel hallway.

Jeff's boat was dark, with only riding lights, these bobbing up and down on the chop an increasing wind was whipping up. I couldn't see his rubber dinghy anywhere along the cobbles, but there was still plenty of shadow in which it could be hidden, as well as considerable bush cover. Most likely he was back on board, in his bunk, that tender deflated and stowed away.

"Left again," the girl said.

It was the road to Brodick, up past the steep golf course. The Avenger went down a gear automatically and I was starting to accelerate when the girl called out.

"Stop! Park on that grass patch to the left."

There was just room to get the car off the tarmac. I switched off the heads. We were overhung by large trees, houses beyond and above, but were still not a great distance from the town.

"Wind down your window."

I did that, letting in wind noise. There wasn't a light to be seen anywhere.

"Get out and stand just beyond the door, holding it open. Don't try to slam it back."

The girl had been taught all the tricks to expect, graduating as a fully qualified pro. I got out, noticing that it was spittering with rain. I stood where I had been told to while she slid over into the driver's seat. I was ordered to turn my back and a moment later there was the click of her shoe on tarmac. We went a few yards up a very dark road and then I got a prod in the spine.

"Left."

We climbed a gradient, through a gap in trees, into an open area the size of a football field, this brightened by today's most lucrative crop, white house trailers. There were four rows of them, many with the dark shapes of cars alongside. Lamlash, which looked so unworldly in spite of a few antique shops, was in the moneymaking business like everyone else, only the town had very sensibly tucked its tourist eyesores out of sight. I couldn't see much to indicate the usual amenities, either: no reception office, certainly no fun and games center, and if there were hot showers these were well hidden. There wasn't a hint of holiday rowdyism on the site, no one staying up all night to drink, and as we skirted the end row of portable cabins these all had mini-curtains pulled as tightly over glass as if they had been suburban villas on a Sunday morning.

My escort kept me well in toward a thick, thorny hedge until we got to the far end of the field, where I was stopped by a trailer so big it would need a truck to move it, probably a quick-return investment belonging to one of those household-ers I had seen drinking on their terraces with sea views. Up in this ghetto you didn't get a view thrown in with your week's rent money, just chipped cups and blankets sent to the cleaners at the end of the season.

I had to mount a box step, open a door, and move into total darkness, but with that gun talking against my spine all the time. The girl shut the door behind us and then switched on lights, not electric, but bottled-gas lamps with pilot jets. The furnishings took on a greenish tinge like the picture from a TV set needing a color transistor panel replaced.

The trailer had two rooms, a sitting room with galley separated from the bedroom by a folding partition, this now closed.

153

In front of it was an artist's easel, empty, and to one side a metal-shaded studio light with a powerful bulb loosely wired to a car battery on the floor. I knew where a picture viewing had taken place.

"Neat arrangement," I said.

"Sit down."

I had a choice of a settee that converted to a bed or one chair by a folding table. The chair was higher than the sofa, so I took that, almost up against a covered sink on which sat a generous collection of bottles—whisky, gin, even vodka, a strange drink to offer in Scotland.

"I could do with something to steady my nerves," I said.

The girl stood looking down at me, one of those hostesses who think it is quite enough to have the stuff on display and who don't pour until practically forced to, so I reached around for a bottle and a glass, at which the gun jerked up to that chin-level position she favored so much. I kept my hand pretty steady while I poured, a too-yellow stream which said cut-price corn whisky with a low malt content. It tasted that way, too.

"You're not joining me?"

She said nothing.

"We're waiting for Hodson to clear all traces of you both out of the hotel and join us?"

She had no comment on that either.

"Angus Kennet rented this for you," I told her. "And he's handy. He fixed up that light. You only went to the hotel because he met you at the ferry with the bad news I was running an active interference on the Renoir deal."

"Think what you like," she said, the gun still up.

I could have thrown my glass, but she would have fired as it left my hand.

A gust shook the trailor, the noise of wind quite loud inside in spite of the padding all around of a blanket blackout. A current of cool air was coming from somewhere. I lifted my eyes as I raised the glass. A roof ventilator had dark paper pasted over it, but had been left a fraction open, presumably to clear out cigarette smoke after a picture-viewing session. There was bound to be some light showing outside from that crack, though I couldn't see what good this was going to do me.

I had to hand it to Angus when it came to the arrangements for a top-secret conference. In an enclosed island community gossip was bound to be a major pastime, based on a practically endless observation of neighbors by neighbors. About the only places where people could come and go all the time unnoticed, strangers in their non-island cars, were the trailer camps. Visitors, being transients, just weren't worth watching, and all the equipment needed for picture viewing would have been easy enough to smuggle in here without causing any comment at all.

The girl in black sat down on the sofa directly opposite, the gun on her knee aimed at my stomach now instead of my head. The attention she was giving me made her somehow reminiscent of a vulture sitting out on a branch waiting for its next meal to die, the same slight hunching of the body suggesting infinite patience.

"Since the picture isn't here, did you tell Mrs. Kennet to take it home again? Because it isn't a Renoir after all?"

She didn't even blink. It occurred to me then that the sound of voices would be likely to leak to the outside world through that crack in the roof, and I'm always an optimist; in a trailer camp there might well be an insomniac out walking around in the rain. If I were walking around in the rain because I couldn't sleep and I heard voices, I'd stop to listen. And if guns were repeatedly mentioned in the talk, I might even be provoked into doing something that went against the usual cautious neutralism of my personality.

"I can't quite understand why you are holding me at gunpoint. Whatever Kennet may have said about me, let me point out that I haven't got a thing against you and Hodson. I mean, of course, if you decided to leave the island without that picture. You can't have people arrested for having an empty suitcase fitted for carrying paintings. So why don't we come to a compromise? I'll forget you were considering buying a valuable commodity from someone who isn't the owner and you forget discovering me in your room damaging a piece of your property. How about that?"

The girl crossed one leg over the other, still with the gun focused on my stomach.

"Did you fall out over price? Lady Eloise keeps up with the art world, but she was well out on the value of Renoirs. She told me hers was worth a quarter of a million. I've got a feeling it was that round sum which provoked the Kennet greed. Perhaps Hodson didn't give them a likely cash price on his first visit; I believe art dealers are cautious about that kind of thing. Incidentally, what was your offer?"

The girl slid the black bag off her left wrist, opened it with that hand, extracted a packet of French cigarettes, shook one out into her mouth, used a lighter, and puffed smoke, all without ever letting the gun muzzle even wobble. If she ever lost an arm she would get along fine. The smoke went straight up to the roof and out the hatch, but she was so dedicated to watching me she didn't seem to notice.

"I've made a simple compromise offer. Don't you believe in compromises?"

She spoke then, one word.

"No."

Vultures don't either. I was beginning to find her even more unnerving in here than when she was prodding me with her small but accurate killing instrument.

"Look," I said. "I'm nothing but a simple tourist who got too curious. It happens all over the world all the time. And quite often the result is being held up at gunpoint like this, but—"

"Shut up!" she said.

What happened next seemed to me to have a positive moral, that garrulity brings its own reward. The door of the trailer had one of those round inset locks that you see on plane johns, nothing projecting in cases of crashes. The extreme caution of whoever was out there planning to come in appeared to rule out Hodson.

A real blast of wind hit us. The door blew open. The girl's head turned. My foot didn't hit her gun, but it did smack hard onto one kneecap just as she swung the muzzle toward a figure in waterproof clothing climbing up and in. There was a bang and a bullet splintered hardboard beside a locker. I had dropped on her before she could fire again. The gun went onto the floor. The girl was a realist; she didn't struggle under me. We both lay sprawled on the sofa, both looking at Jeff.

He had come ashore to follow me, prepared for everything, including bad weather, waterproof clothing strapped onto the scooter's carrier. He was swathed in this from hat to midcalf, practically a total disguise. I admired his reaction to being shot at: he turned to look at a piece of split paneling before he looked at us, then kicked the door shut. The wind was now making so much noise that I didn't think any of the other campers likely to have been disturbed by the sound of a lady's handgun. Before I unwound myself from my captive, I used one foot to kick the gun over to Jeff, who bent and picked it up, then slid it into a pocket equipped with a flap.

I couldn't see him very well in that green light with his face shaded by the brim of the hat, though his mustache stuck out with beads of damp on it, but I had the feeling at once that he was one of those who really need eight hours' sleep every night to keep their charm going. He had come here without it. He took off his hat and shook it.

"There's free drink if you'd like one," I said.

The look he gave me then suggested that a relationship which had seemed to start so well had suddenly moved into a terminal phase. Then he stared at the girl in black. She stared back, hunched up on the sofa again. While they were both at it, I reached over and picked up the black handbag, opening it and emptying the contents on the table in front of me.

Her wallet was in a state of bad repair, probably a sentimental souvenir from the days when she had been poor but honest. Inside was enough money in notes of large denominations to start a small business, mostly pounds, but also some francs and a pack of lire with a rubber band around it. The passport photograph identified a Miss Lilias Stokouros of Beirut, a Lebanese citizen. In the picture she had a long haircut from a central parting which was far from chic, suggesting an earlier phase when her weekend sport might well have been placard carrying in protest marches. I held out the travel document to Jeff.

"I've got a feeling she belongs to the art world. Does that name mean anything to you?"

He stepped forward to take the passport, staring at it.

"No. Never heard of her."

Miss Stokouros had now made a tight parcel of herself on the sofa, giving an impression she was waiting for something, probably Hodson.

"Bolt the door, Jeff."

He did that.

"I don't think she was born in Lebanon," I said. "The place is a racial melting pot as well as being a useful convenience address. What was your name before you changed it, Miss Stokouros?"

She had now discovered that ventilator, her eyes on it, but had nothing to say. I got up and closed the thing, to prevent further leakage, then took up a checkbook printed for Mustapha Aziz and Company against an account with the Banque Internationale de L'Orient Midi of Beirut. Just one check had been used. On the stub were figures, nothing else: "160,000." I handed the book to Jeff.

"I suppose that means Lebanese pounds?"

"I'd think so."

"How much in British money?"

An auctioneer's provincial man needed only seconds to work out values in any foreign currency.

"About thirty thousand."

"Mustapha Aziz and Company mean anything to you?"

"I'm trying to think. I've never had any dealings with the Middle East but . . ."

Jeff might have shut down the charm output but his brain was still functioning. After about twenty seconds he said:

"Yes! The Carpaccio!"

Miss Stokouros's gaze at a ventilator was broken. Carpaccio meant something to her. All he meant to me was that he was Italian and a painter, but then my educational tours in Europe had all been under the auspices of my father, who was much more interested in restaurants and women than in painting.

"It was only months after the doubling of the Middle East oil prices. We get this company news sheet of the big sales—"

"Push nearer the point, Jeff!"

Stokouros was now looking at him.

"The point is that I'm damn sure it was a man from Mustapha Aziz and Company, representing an unknown buyer, who paid a record price for a Carpaccio. That inflated the market on Venetians. At a time when prices had been dropping wildly. Though, of course, not many Carpaccios come up for sale."

"What's the take-home price of one if you can lay your hands on it?"

"They have reached a quarter of a million. These days you'd have to take fifty thousand off that."

Realists, these boys, quite prepared for big commission cuts in recession years. But if you've built up their kind of fat in the good times, you can afford to hibernate through the bad. It was being borne in on me that I'd been a fool to waste my life making diesel engines against cutthroat Japanese competition. It still mightn't be too late to set up as the Far East's number one Ming and Tang hunter.

"Can you remember any other dealings between your company and Mustapha Aziz?"

"Not offhand. But a private buyer probably wouldn't use the same agents twice . . . if he's going for investment only."

"Investment only is the same as building up a store of gold bricks in your cellar? You don't want gossip about it?"

"That's right."

"What percentage of your big deals are with people buying for investment?"

"Hard to say. But real art lovers don't often have the big money."

"The Arabs have billions they can't get rid of. Jeff, would it surprise you to learn that there's a vast air-conditioned storehouse of European painting somewhere in the middle of the Arabian desert?"

"How could a little thing like that surprise me these days?"

It was still quite a thought. The pure faith of Islam doesn't allow any representation of the human form in its artwork. I had a vision of an orthodox Mohammedan oil sheik refusing to look at a Monet picnic he had just bought for around a million, instead having it rushed under covers to a Middle Eastern equivalent of Fort Knox.

Stokouros now wasn't able to disguise her interest, and she was staring at Jeff like a women's liberationist up against a really prime specimen of male pig. It was quite a relief to have that heat off me.

"How did you track us down to this trailer?" I asked. "Noticed my car parked by the road?"

"No."

Jeff suddenly decided to risk alcohol on an empty stomach just before dawn, reaching across the table for a bottle and a glass. He was pouring when he said:

"Followed you here from the hotel."

"To which you had followed me from the Kennets'?"

"Not at once."

"You were looking for a green Mini and a blonde?"

"Yes."

"Did you find them?"

"No."

"I don't want you to think I'm not grateful for the way you keep showing up when I need you. At the same time I can't get away from the feeling that you think I have a cash interest in this painting deal. Do you?"

"Maybe."

"If you saw me being escorted to my car at the point of a gun and listened outside here, you ought to realize by this time that Miss Stokouros and I are not allies."

"It is my information that you work on your own."

I was getting just a little heated. "Look, I'm a businessman, not an international crook!"

Jeff remained completely composed. "That seems to be a matter of opinion," he said. "Your arrival on Arran just a day or two before Hodson showed up was an interesting coincidence."

I stared at him. "How did you know that Hodson was on this island?"

He sipped whisky. "I recognized him when I was waiting at your hotel for you to arrive. Drinking bad beer, you remember?"

"But you'd never *seen* Hodson."

"No. In London they gave me a blown-up snapshot of him. He's shaved off his mustache and his hair's longer, but when he got out of the Audi with this girl I was pretty sure he was my man. I went into the bar later and had a good look at him. It was Hodson, all right."

"You suspected he'd come to the hotel for contact with me?"

"Logical, wasn't it? It seems he had."

"Only because Angus had warned him and this girl that I had been snooping around Tigh-na-Claddach."

"So you say."

I didn't shout, but I wanted to. "When I start stealing oil

paintings, they will all be in the half million and above price range."

He smiled. It wasn't a sudden switch-on of the charm. "You might be getting the feel for a new field of operation with a more modest deal. A trial run?"

"So you think my fight with Kennet was a case of thieves falling out?"

"Could be."

I turned to the girl.

"Miss Stokouros, will you tell this man that you had neither heard of nor seen me before you landed on Arran?"

She didn't tell Jeff anything, but she had switched that steady gaze back to me, acutely interested in the news that Angus and I had been fighting.

"All this excitement has gone to my bladder," I said. "You'll have to excuse me while I step outside."

For a moment Jeff wasn't going to let me open that door, then he decided to go on playing me on a long line, slackening off the reel again like the true sportsman he was. I walked across the floor, pulled back a bolt, and went out into the storm.

Jeff had wheeled his scooter up from the entrance to the camp and left it leaning against the end of the trailer. If Hodson had been here and seen that machine, he had decided not to come in. I began to run toward the waiting Avenger. It was within minutes of a gloomy new day.

TEN

Brodick was storm-battered under thin gray light, palms in the hotel gardens turned into broken ribbed umbrellas, looking as alien to this environment as lions in an Icelandic zoo. I punched buttons on the car radio but the British Broadcasting Corporation was still asleep, and the Continental stations refused to give me a weather forecast. My estimate of wind force was eight or nine, increasing fast. The rain had stopped, but enormous black clouds were being ripped open by the peak of Goat Fell, re-forming on the other side, making for the mainland to soak Ayrshire. The estuary was gray, flecked with white, spume screens being carried for miles. Beyond the town the shore road gave me a close-up of eight-foot waves crashing on rocks, these now on a receding tide, but promising to come back at the flood, really angry.

I was just south of Corrie when a torn cloud, unable to seal itself up again, emptied its entire contents in wind-driven torrents. It was one of those roads, all bends, which Highlanders drive over at sixty, and with a high survival rate, but it needs steel nerves and specialist training, knowing exactly what to do when you meet a tourist car head on around a corner to make certain that the visitors die, not you. Visibility was so poor through frantic wipers that I cut back to forty, then thirty. It was a good thing I had; a projectile shot out from behind a buttress. I saw a man's face beyond a windshield, recognized it, then we both hit undrained water, sending up speedboat sheets of spray. I fought the Avenger up onto a grass shoulder and back onto slimy tarmac, expecting a scream of tearing metal. This didn't come. My mirror showed a green Mini flipping its rear end out of a half skid, violent acceleration part of the recovery.

Angus had been alone. I could have turned and given chase, but had little chance of catching up with even a battered GT 1250 driven by a man whose mental balance was suspect. He might spin around and come after me. I drove on, waiting for an angry buzzing astern as he came up in a bid to pass, then ditched me. Bend after bend went by with nothing in the mirror.

The barred gate at Tigh-na-Claddach had been left wide open. I cut the engine in front of the house, to a takeover of wind noise, that canyon between overhanging mountains acting as a funnel with this place set in the middle of its mouth, and I got out into a roaring that was like full tide in a sea cave. Cyclonic gusts came sweeping down the driveway, and the plantation trees were humble, bowing low.

Unless someone had left a window open, it wasn't an easy place to get into. I knocked and rang for all of five minutes before the door seemed suddenly to surrender to wind, an invading gust sweeping me into the vestibule and then rushing on to set doors banging. I put my shoulder against solid oak and had to shove hard to get it shut again, scarcely seeing Anne in the process. It was dark inside, and they were saving electricity, no lights on in the hall.

"You have private hurricanes," I said. "Down the coast it's only moving toward force ten."

That got no response. Her face was a light patch in gloom. I was halfway down the hall toward a glow from the sitting room when she called out:

"What do you want?"

"The answers to some questions."

"Oh . . . *God!*"

The log fire was beyond reviving, a heap of gray ash. There was gray at the windows, too. Only one lamp was lit. There was the smell of stale cigarette smoke and a good many glasses of whisky poured. One had half an inch left in it, not my idea of breakfast.

Anne didn't follow me at once. It wouldn't have been a total surprise to see her come in carrying Angus's gun, with the telescopic sight still attached to the barrel, but she came with empty hands, moving slowly around one of those British doors that have the hinges on the wrong side, screening the room to which they give access. Her hair hadn't been combed for some time and I hadn't shaved; there was a feeling between us like the heavy disillusionment of long habit. She moved as far as the nearest table and took a cigarette pack from it, striking a match, not looking at me. Her trouser suit was crumpled.

We were both waiting, I with a sense of fear or shock having almost completely eroded the personality presented to me only a day or two ago in this room. Now I was being given a physical presence, nothing else, as though she were prisoner and I the prosecutor. I had to play my role.

"You've been a party to stealing your mother's Renoir."

She stared at a rug. "Is that what you think?"

"There's a considerable heap of evidence. I've just come from a woman called Stokouros. For some time she kept a gun shoved against my side."

I had expected some reaction from that, but I didn't get one. Smoke dribbled away from Anne's nostrils and mouth.

"I passed your husband on the road. Where is he going? To answer a sudden SOS from Hodson?"

"I don't know."

"That's a pretty bloody improbable answer!"

"It's the truth."

"Has there been a phone call here within the last hour?"

"Yes. Angus took it."

"And you don't know what it was about?"

"No."

She went to a chair and sat, staring at another rug, the burn-marked Persian, which wouldn't fetch much at a sale of the contents of this house.

"He's left me," Anne said.

"That's great! He's left you. To ride round and round the island in a green Mini until he gets hungry? Because he's not going to get off Arran today. No one is. So can you do better than that, please? Where has your husband gone?"

"I've told you, I don't know! I don't expect . . ."

She was back to that habit of allowing sentences to die half-way.

"What don't you expect?"

"Ever to see him again."

"Packed his things, has he?"

"A suitcase."

Anne was sitting back in the chair now, not looking at me. Sunken springs forced her body into a parody of relaxation and, as though to complete this, she let her head fall against the back, fair hair away from both sides of her face. She seemed to be staring at cracks in the plaster ceiling.

"One suitcase and the Renoir?"

"The picture is over in Mother's house."

Her eyes moved to see how I took that.

"You don't need to believe me," she said. "The key to the bungalow is on the mantelshelf."

I found the key and went out of the room, down the hall, leaving the front door lock with the catch up, fighting my way across the wide stretch of grass. Half shelter on the porch of Eloise's house was like standing on a station platform when an express roars through.

The sitting room was shrouded by lowered blinds. The last

time I had seen this place it looked like the saloon bar in a Western after the big fight; now it was tidy. A dented bronze incense burner was back on top of the bookcase, though a bad piece of scarring on the doorjamb, white paint chipped off, hadn't been dealt with yet. There was no trace of a shattered red chair and in the bedroom the coverlet had been changed, suitcases put back up on the bed. A heap of blood-soaked towels was gone. Back in the sitting room again, I switched on a painting's private light, staring for all of a minute. The uncloying sweetness of Renoir's women didn't seem to be there, that shining joy was gone.

I ripped the phone cord from its baseboard connection, then went out into the storm again. Wind had done a lot more to Anne's roses than just breaking off the flowering stems. The bushes themselves were loosened in sodden earth, only the tap roots holding, the plants tossed from side to side in holes that could have been troweled out. When the violence was over the entire bed would be a horticultural casualty ward. Up against the house, a rambler was sending out flapped May Day calls for help which I didn't think would be coming. I shut out two-thirds of the noise and went down a hall smelling of coffee.

Anne had made a quite remarkable recovery, which included an attempt to establish a kind of domestic norm, switching from whisky therapy for shock to a fresh brew in a pot and a plate of homemade biscuits. There was a cup for me and she was already holding hers, having moved to a chair with better springs, upright now, sipping. I went to the fireplace, picked up a poker, stirring those ashes.

"That's out," she said.

"I'm just looking to see if you've been burning red lacquer recently."

"What?" She put down her cup. Coffee had slopped into the saucer.

"The chair your mother used as a table. And a ladder. It's gone. What was left of it."

"What are you talking about?"

"Evidence got rid of. Have you been over to the cottage since the accident?"

"No."

"Then someone else is house-proud. The place has all been tidied up. Including a lot of bloody towels."

"I don't know what . . ."

"Who put the picture back over there?"

"Angus. But . . ."

"That red chair had been fixed so that it would collapse when your mother stood on it. Ingenious. After the accident it was glued together again."

She was staring. "Glued . . . ?"

She pushed herself upright. We stood facing each other.

"You're making this up!"

"He didn't tell you about our fight in the bungalow? During it he came at me with that Dayak chopper in his hands. He meant to kill."

"I won't believe this! I won't! It can't be true!"

"How did your husband account for four inches of plaster back from his forehead into his scalp?"

"He . . . fell. Out on the rocks. We have a creel. For lobsters. He was going to it."

"At night?"

"He sometimes does. With a light. It depends on the tides."

From the look in her eyes now I could almost believe her.

"He's a tough customer. I thought that knock on the head would keep him immobile for hours."

"You . . . did it?"

"No, he fell. In the sitting room over there. Lucky for me he did, too. You'd better sit down again."

I had to half push her into the chair. She brought both hands up and hid her face. Her breathing suddenly began to rasp.

"You didn't help your mother pack yesterday. So what did you do?"

"I . . . can't talk."

That asthma was too sudden.

"What did you do?"

"Headache. I came back and lay down."

"Leaving everything to Angus. Did he carry over that luggage from the storeroom next to his workshop?"

She nodded, still with her hands up.

"So your mother allowed him in her bungalow?"

"There was no one else . . . to do it."

Two big suitcases and a cabin trunk meant more than one trip, giving Angus plenty of time to carry the chair to his workshop, do the necessary on it, and return it to its usual place. Eloise might have asked him to lift down the picture and if she had he had conveniently forgotten. I could see her propped up against pillows in that bed, hating the sound of his feet in her rooms, hating it even more when he came into the bedroom with the luggage, an invasion of her sacred privacy just endured.

"You'd like a whisky?" I asked.

She lowered her hands and shook her head, staring at the ashes in the fire.

"Were you in bed until the accident?"

"Yes."

"When he called you where was he?"

She was still having difficulty with her breathing, the sound of it making a duet with the ticking of the mock-ormolu clock. It took a long time for her answer to come.

"He was in the garden. He heard . . . the crash."

"He'd been waiting to hear it."

Her head moved in protest.

"You ran over? Was Angus in the bungalow when you got there?"

"Yes. She was on the floor. We didn't move her. We phoned."

"Did you see that chair she'd used? Was it in two pieces?"

"I don't remember."

She shook her head again. I'm not good at interrogations, that trick of quietly maneuvering your victims into a corner before you really start to hit them hard. I had got Anne into a corner, all right, but I couldn't manage the follow-through. Whatever she was feeling—shock, terror, pain—was contained for all that shortened, sucked-in breathing. She didn't cry, just sat hunched over looking at ashes until I had to stop her doing that. I went out and found sticks in a cupboard off the back passage from the kitchen, and a newspaper, returning to light the fire, bending down to pump away with bellows until there were flames to color her face as she stared at them. I threw on some logs. After that I had some cold coffee out of the pot. I offered her a cigarette, but she gave no sign that she had heard, her withdrawal now as total as a manic-depressive's in the black phase. The wheezing went on. I sat down opposite and began again.

"Anne, you knew that Hodson thought your mother's painting was a Renoir."

It seemed a long time before she spoke.

"No. He said . . . it might be."

"He was convinced enough to bring a client carrying a checkbook to this island. And that client wrote out a check after seeing the picture."

"Yes."

"I've just come from the trailer. I know how carefully everything was set up. Who did that? Your husband?"

"Yes."

"But it was you who picked up Stokouros and Hodson outside my hotel and took them to the trailer."

"Yes."

"Why?"

"I wouldn't let Angus do it."

"So you have that check for something like thirty thousand pounds?"

She looked at me for the first time in long enough. "No, I don't."

170

"You gave it to Angus?"

"No. I wouldn't take it. The woman . . . tore it up."

"You wouldn't take that check because the price wasn't right? You'd been expecting a lot more?"

"No."

"Why weren't you willing to sell when you'd gone to all the trouble of bringing Hodson here and having the trailer ready?"

"I didn't! It was Angus. No, that's not true. I let them go on with it. But . . ."

"Answer me, Anne! Why did you say no to thirty thousand pounds in that trailer?"

"The picture wasn't mine to sell! It was Mother's!"

"Bit late in the day to go moral, wasn't it?"

"I knew you wouldn't believe me."

"I'd still like to hear your story."

"I never believed the painting was worth anything. But I've lived with nothing but Mother's talk about it ever since we had that man here. I let Angus go on with things because I wanted to prove to him that he was just dreaming about that money."

"So it was a shock when you found out a short time ago that he wasn't dreaming?"

"Yes."

"Why was it you who took the picture to the trailer?"

"I couldn't let Angus do it. Or come with me. He'd have been determined to sell it, whatever I said. And when I came back here with the picture and told him what had happened—that I wasn't going to sell it—I thought . . ."

"What did you think, Anne?"

"He wanted to kill me. He looked . . . mad."

The phone rang in the hall. Anne was up before me, but my chair was nearer the door.

"I'll take it," I said.

She stood there, wanting to protest. I went into the hall, shutting the door to the sitting room behind me.

Jeff was in a call box somewhere, demanding that I identify

myself before he pressed a button and lost his money. The message he sent over a line cleared between us was simple.

"I knew you'd be there, you bastard."

I take abuse without flinching—people are always misinterpreting my motivations—but I was a bit surprised this time because I couldn't believe that he had been expecting me to come back into that trailer. His anger, traveling over that wire like an explosion, wasn't really directed at me, or not most of it.

"That bitch kicked me into the water!"

He hadn't been near water when I left him, but it seemed he was very wet now, and when he wasn't talking I could hear his teeth chattering like castanets.

"I made her row the dinghy. With that chop on, it was hard going. Took us a long time."

"What were you taking her to your boat for, Jeff?"

"Because my anchor was on a soft bottom. I knew it would be dragging in a wind of this force. I had to get out there. The only thing to do was take her, since you'd run off."

"Then what happened?"

"I damn nearly drowned, that's what. I was in all this waterproof gear. I couldn't get the zips undone. I had to swim in. I'm bloody lucky to have made it."

"But how did Stokouros kick you into the harbor?"

"I'll tell you how. She looked absolutely exhausted from that rowing. I didn't want her to do it, but you can't row and hold a gun. When we got out to the cruiser she looked absolutely all in. Couldn't haul herself up into the cockpit, was straddled between the dinghy and the boat, holding on to a stanchion. I had to stand up to give her a lift, which wasn't easy with that water boiling around us. And that was when she put one foot in my face and shoved."

Jeff coughed, and then went on with an epic account of a three-hundred-yard swim wearing twenty pounds of clothing. I cut through that.

"Is Stokourous still sitting out on your cruiser?"

"Sitting in it? She got the engine on and the anchor up in about two minutes. She knows all about boats, that one. Brought it past me while I was wallowing around trying to keep afloat."

"Where was she going?"

"Straight out to sea. By the north entrance to the bay."

"Into that weather?"

"Yes. Right into it. Last I saw of the riding lights, she was through the channel."

"Jeff, it'll be really dirty out there now."

"Are you telling me?"

He must have walked the girl down to his boat from the trailer camp, which made it practically dead certain that Hodson would have seen them. It had been Hodson who had phoned here, telling Angus to meet him someplace, probably Brodick.

"Stokouros won't try to make for the mainland in this," I said. "She hasn't got the picture; she doesn't have to run away from anything."

"What are you getting at?"

"That she'll be trying for a rendezvous with Hodson. And probably Angus. Which means Brodick. The wind's westerly. If she hugs the coast going north she'll get there all right. And probably soon. Hodson has the Audi; he can keep the boat in view from high ground. As soon as he sees where she's making for, he'll join her. Get me?"

"Yes. I've got my scooter. I'll meet her, too!"

"I'm coming. Only you'll be there long before I am. Listen, Jeff. Don't do anything on your own. Have you got that gun?"

"Have I, hell. I had to put it down to help her. As soon as she had the cruiser under way she pulled in the dinghy, hauled it up and deflated it."

"So she has the gun?"

"Yes, unless it fell out."

"She'll have it. Which means you wait for me by the dock gates. Keep hidden until I show up. No matter how tempted you may be to start something on your own. Understand?"

"All right."

I hung up, then ripped the phone cord from its connection box. There was no sign of a lead to an upstairs extension.

Anne was standing on the hearth rug. I kept one hand on the doorknob.

"If you met your husband at the Brodick ferry yesterday, he didn't come off that boat. Because he was already on the island, getting about on a bicycle, I should imagine. Does he have a bicycle?"

She just stared at me.

"If he wasn't in bed in that playroom of his upstairs, he was using his other playroom out back. Sleeping in a camper's bag on the floor. Your mother didn't trip and fall into that rose bed. She was chopped from behind. And you suspected that he had done just that."

Anne didn't move.

"The picture over in the bungalow is a substitution. Part of your deal with Hodson. He was to have that painted by some hack and bring it to the island so that when your mother started to bleat about the painting on her wall not being *her* Renoir you had a beautiful out. She'd had a phobia about that picture for years, was more than slightly deranged on the subject. Even the doctor would have believed you. I'm the only one you can't sell that to."

Anne swayed a little then, as though losing control of balance. On the way to the front door I heard something that put ice on my spine. The asthmatic had started to scream.

Outside the rain was streaking down. As I was getting into my car, Rufus, above wind noise, was howling from an outbuilding somewhere, a wild, dismal sound, as though the dog sensed death on the prowl.

This time I got a weather report from a punched button. The storm had reached force twelve in some areas, gusting to ninety

174

miles an hour in Kintyre and south Arran. The worst wasn't over yet, either; there were warnings out for the whole of Scotland and much of northern England. Three ships were in trouble off the Irish coast, including a two-hundred-thousand-ton tanker, and in the North Sea one of the legs of a ten-million-pound oil rig had buckled. All this disturbance was allegedly part of hurricane Susannah, which had ravaged the New England coast, then taken a brief rest before coming hurtling across the Atlantic, picking up support en route from a rogue polar air stream. The newscaster sounded depressed enough to have been giving out the results of a world congress of financial experts in Washington.

I hit Brodick's esplanade at a speed considerably in excess of the limit, risking a skid on greasy asphalt. The tide was well back, about on the turn, but in spite of this, wind-driven waves were sending spray over the end of the ferry pier. Beyond the breakwater it looked as though a giant eggbeater had been at work, froth everywhere, much of this probably whipped-up effluent from cities along the estuary. Farther out, huge seas took over, and the crest of one pushed up a boat, stern on to me. I didn't really identify it on that first quick look, but when it rose again I did, mainly from large areas of glass. It was Jeff's cruiser, leaving Brodick after a brief stopover, headed now due east toward the Scottish coast.

The town's shopping area was empty, everything still shut, the tail sting of a transatlantic hurricane, with its pressure jets of rain and whirling gusts for scrubbers, as ruthless as a car wash. Beyond the dock gates, in an exposed parking area, rows of cars abandoned by their owners were under vicious assault. A loosened tarpaulin flapped like a sail from a big lorry and in the inner harbor the radar-hung masts of a couple of moored fishing boats swayed over deserted decks. The whole area looked like a factory closed by a lightning strike.

I spotted the Audi in one of the queues for a morning ferry which wasn't going to come, but I had to drive around to locate the green Mini, finding this up against a shed. I put the Avenger behind it and got out, wind attacking me like a boxer going for the knockout. I went around a corner of the shed, head down, and almost fell over a motor scooter lying on its side. About five yards away, humped against a door marked "Enquiries," was the shape of a man. Wind had taken his hat and hair identified him.

Jeff was breathing, unmarked, no blood. He might have been catching up on lost sleep out here in the rain. When he came around it would be with a very stiff neck. I knew who had chopped him.

He wasn't an easy lift. It took minutes to get him around to my car and then lever him up onto the back seat. I left him curled on this, looking like a man whose subconscious keeps telling him that it is Sunday morning and he doesn't have to wake up. I went to collect the scooter, just managing to fit this into the trunk, but with the lid up, flapping and threatening to take off.

On the road to Lamlash, up on high ground, I was facing into the wind and I risked stopping for a moment to look back. Jeff's boat was now about two miles out into the firth, clear of any shelter from Arran and smacking into the really big seas, surrounded by almost permanent spray clouds. Even with the wind astern, the cruiser was going to have one hell of a fight to get over to the mainland, many hours in the crossing, which gave me plenty of time for a report to the police later in circumstances which wouldn't be embarrassing for either Jeff or me. In the dim daylight I located the dinghy drawn well up on the cobbles by Lamlash Bay and I unloaded the scooter there, leaving it against a tree, then drove on to the hotel.

In the drive Jeff came around, perhaps as a result of one of the bumps. He said "Hell" first, then gave a yelp like a dog kicked. By the time I had parked he was half sitting up, one hand probing the back of his neck.

"Karate chop," I said. "From a golfer who plays other games as well."

His eyes were a migraine sufferer's, out of focus. I think he saw two Paul Harrises.

"Why the hell didn't you wait for me, Jeff?"

"No," he said.

I got him out of the car and held him by the elbows while he was very sick into the edge of the hayfield. After this he seemed slightly more mobile, but keeping him upright was like trying to support an outsize soaked sponge. I helped him into a front hall dedicated to that soundless emptiness which was the big feature of this hotel, except when the proprietor used his pistol, then to the stairs. Jeff took each tread of these like an old man whose prospects of ever coming down them again on his own feet are thin, and we had a long rest break on the half landing. I hadn't really noticed as we passed it that the door to the bar was open, and certainly there had been no noises coming out of that big room. There were now, a sloshing sound that could only come from a very wet mop, and a moment later this was accompanied by a thin, clear woman's voice.

She was singing a Malay pantun, a verse form tending to the obscene, but this one more subtle than most. I heard the words very clearly, as it had been intended I should.

> "A bangle on the wrist is the fashion,
> But I wear mine another way.
> People tell me to curb my passion—
> What do I care what people say?"

Aishah awarded herself a repeat encore as we began to climb again, the words higher pitched and much louder. The little bitch had seen us arrive and was mocking me.

> "Banyak orang larang jangan—
> Sahaya sa-orang turut hati?"

I got Jeff into my bedroom and shut the door. He stood droop-ing while I got him out of waterproof clothing. Underneath this he was really wet. Propped against the bed, he was able to help somewhat with the stripping process, shivering like a diver who has stayed too long under Antarctic ice. Wind was blowing straight at us from a paneless window. When he was finally in dry trousers and a sweater, I pushed him under the covers, where he lay staring at the ceiling, vision coming back to nor-mal.

"Why the hell didn't you wait for me?" I asked.

He thought about this, then said, "She was bumping my boat."

"What?"

"Holding it on engines. Against the pier. No fenders out."

"You mean the tin was getting dented? You risked being killed for that?"

"I didn't . . ."

He abandoned a sentence, as though there was no point in trying to explain the deep love that develops between a man and the boat for which he has paid a lot of money.

"Did you see who was in the cockpit?"

"Stokouros and Hodson."

"No sign of Kennet?"

Jeff tried to shake his head, but it hurt him.

"He chopped you," I said. "Must have come up behind. What were you doing? Starting to run toward your boat?"

"I saw the Mini. I went past it around the end of the shed."

"Which means you'd been riding around in that parking area advertising yourself."

"Well . . . maybe. I saw my boat in. From the hill. I couldn't wait for you. They were going out again. But I don't know where Kennet was."

"I'll tell you where he was. In a phone box. Trying to get a message through to his wife about a change in their plans. You probably rode right past him. So he followed."

Jeff continued to stare at the ceiling, then he said, "I'm going to be sick again."

Ten minutes later I went down the stairs to organize some room service for the patient. There was a big area of wet boarding between me and a girl being generous with the water but sparing with energy expended in spreading it about. Aishah was wearing a pair of dark ski pants and an old blue sweater out at the elbows, black hair pulled tight by a piece of string at the back of her neck. She looked remarkably like a sampan woman in the river under my Singapore apartment, cleaning up the deck of her floating home. She didn't see me until she turned to plop the mop back in the bucket, but then she let go of the handle and stood to return my stare. After a moment she lifted one hand to wipe sweat away from her forehead. Then she smiled.

It was the smile of a child reacting to the sudden appearance of a companion with whom she shares a secret, the rest of the world shut away by their closed complicity in this. I was just about to smile back when there was a bang which shook every loose-framed window in the building, loud enough to be a World War II mine going off thirty years behind schedule.

ELEVEN

The Avenger's progress down a disintegrating track was blocked by a white police car and a blue coast guard Land-Rover. As I got out, a policeman came around from sheltering behind the Ford, young, with long fair hair flowing out from under the cap, a recruit from the Outer Hebrides who had probably spoken Gaelic at home, his English learned as a second language. His voice was gentle and his idioms shaky.

"You will not be getting down this track, sir. And that is an order."

It didn't really sound like an order. Looking at him, rosy-cheeked in a howling gale and a winter temperature, I couldn't believe he had ever arrested anyone in a career that was unlikely to be more than a year old. When pressed, he explained who had issued the order. It was his sergeant, whom it was clear he feared almost as much as his United Free Presbyterian God. He was a nice boy the world would harden up soon enough, and this seemed a pity.

"It is for the ambulance, sir. To keep the road clear so that people will not be coming."

I told him why I wanted down that path.

"But we thought it was an English visitor's boat, sir."

"It's almost certainly an Argyll boat. From Crinan."

That made all the difference.

"Great heavens! The sergeant will be wanting to know this."

"I'll take the word to him. But you'll have to let me park."

"Whatever would an Argyll boat be doing out in this?"

"Stolen," I said.

Crime still shocked him. There was another bang, the fifth since the one that had shaken the hotel's windows.

"They'll be having a terrible job to get the line on her, sir, with the wind. A cyclone it is now."

"Have you seen the boat that's hit?"

"No, sir. I was to stay here. It's about a mile up the track. There is a great rock that sticks up in the channel. The boat's to the lee side of that, so the coast guard was telling me."

I went back to the Avenger. Jeff was sitting with his head sunk down on his chest. Hunched over, and in my clothes, he looked like a man being brought home after a too good night with the boys.

"You can't make it," I said. "It's quite a walk."

"I'm coming."

I got in and bumped the car forward.

"Jeff, there's a not a damn thing you can do. And it may not be your boat. Some idiot yachtsman. The coast watcher I phoned hadn't been able to see her."

"It's my boat, all right."

The young policeman showed me where to park. He was anxious again.

"You'll be telling the sergeant why I have been letting you go down?"

"I'll do that."

Jeff, ignoring the law, had already started along the path. I caught up with him. He was walking with his head down, like a man trying to keep the rain from his face, though there was now no rain, just the beating wind and sea testing rocks. He seemed quite able to resist gust assaults, not allowing them to deflect him, plodding on.

The path started to rise, but we were still screened from the Firth of Clyde by an upthrust of rocky ground and couldn't see what the wind was doing to open water. Behind us, in Lamlash Bay, the play craft reared and bucked against anchor chains like newly captured wild horses. As we came up on the rise I appreciated what the policeman had said about a cyclone; the wind was no longer from the west but was circling to come blasting up from the Irish Sea. The undertone of noise was that steady, unbroken roar which defines the difference between gale and storm. This was storm, all right.

We saw the rock first as a black peak sticking up out of a mist of spray. Then a huge breaking wave seemed to wash it clean right down to the base. At that base, and opposite the Arran shore, was what was left of a boat.

Jeff stopped dead. I don't think his thought then was for people in that boat, and mine wasn't either. It was the wreck itself that shocked, a hull still resisting, not much else left. We didn't have much of a look before the spume mist rose again, but long enough for identification, and I could see why whoever had been at the helm of Jeff's boat had chosen to run in between the rock and the Arran coast, for even at a still lowish tide there was a current-propelled smoothness of water there, in sharp contrast to what was beyond—waves broken by a change in wind direction, great swells that had been driving steadily away toward the east now with their tops chopped off to form new waves riding north over the tumbled heaps of the old. The cruiser, running through the narrow channel, must first have grounded, then been swung off course by a swirl of the current, then been sucked over onto an invisible ledge at the base of the rock. That it was up on a shelf was obvious, the hull almost over on its starboard side. While we watched, a great clump of water snatched from a swell smashed against the pinnacle of rock to waterfall down on the wreck.

Well below us a huddle of coast guard men with their gear were at work on a strip of cobble beach, with two policemen standing by. Jeff started down, in a shamble that was almost a run. The island screening Lamlash Bay no longer gave any shelter from a wind gone southerly, the blast without any pulse through it of ebb, then strength again, but steady, unvarying aggression. The only noise getting through wind roar was the thud of waves, but even these huge explosions against rocks reached me as not much more than a gentle extra palpitation on eardrums.

I was halfway down the slope when I saw that the last rocket had got a line over the boat, and this had been secured, the lead wire for the breeches buoy already being tightened. It was like watching telephone linesmen working through a snowstorm, the men at the far end of the operation invisible. Jeff turned his head to shout something back at me, but I didn't hear one word. Directly over the rock, weirdly immune to what was happening beneath, a ballet of sea gulls dove and zoomed up again through spray, but the screeching that went with that aerial dance was blotted out.

Jeff made for one of the policemen, who swung around, astonished first, then apparently angry. They leaned toward each other for a shouting match, then Jeff pointed out toward the boat. Spray dropped over them and over the men on the winding gear.

When this cleared I saw the cruiser for seconds, the hull still apparently intact, but the mast gone, the bridge crushed, a canopy over the stern cockpit completely torn away. Bridge roofing had been jammed down on bent supports, covering the hatch to the cabin. Every scrap of that toughened glass which had made the boat's upper works look like a series of stepped greenhouses had gone. I could only make out one figure crouched down amidships, a man pulling on the rope bringing out the canvas cradle.

Solid water came over the pinnacle of the rock again and before the spray from this dropped another wave followed. For what seemed to be minutes the cruiser was hidden, but the line to it started to sag from a weight suddenly put on. Jeff and I joined the team of oilskinned coast guards to pull, six of us fighting a tidal surge in the channel. A bundle swirled in the foam and a couple of the men went out to the thighs in water, grabbing it. What was finally hauled out of a suck-back was just identifiable as the man I had seen once in a hotel bar. There was blood on his face, his mouth was open, his eyes shut.

The ambulance men had arrived, three of them, who apparently decided that artificial respiration wasn't called for on the spot. Hodson was parceled in a blanket and rolled onto a stretcher for the carry along the track. I helped them with their load up the steepest part of the gradient and was turning back toward the wreck when I saw something well out in the firth which twanged the chords of old fears.

I had seen it twice before, a freak sea thrown up by a sudden change in wind direction, the product of two waves colliding that fuse instead of breaking each other up, producing a monster which looks as though it had been fathered by an undersea volcanic eruption. The thing coming at us was ten to twelve feet higher than any of the other waves, a moving hill ironing out all rivals, uncrested, its summit almost smooth.

I got down to the shore fast, grabbing at a coast guard's arm. He spun around, ready to tell off a rubbernecking visitor. I pointed. He looked out toward the firth. The others heard that shout. What we all did then was almost pure reflex. The line to the wreck slackened off on a spinning drum; then as the harness disappeared the gear was dragged off cobbles up onto the rocks behind.

The great wave had even flattened out those ahead of it, and the wreck was reprieved from those recurring waterfalls. We saw the man still on her waving, not understanding why he had been abandoned, while behind him and the black rock the monster seemed to be taking its time, glistening green and black, with rivulets of white marble beginning to streak its flanks. Only yards from the rock, it seemed to pause, swelling even more. Then it broke. The roar cracked in the channels of my ears. The rock disappeared, the cruiser buried under a Niagara, the cobbles where we had been standing covered by a vast surge of foam which reached for the rocks on which we stood now.

The suck-back was vicious, taking with it half a beach of groaning stones. Spray stung like sleet. When I saw the cruiser again it had been swept off the ledge well out into the estuary, stern and cockpit under water, only a few feet of bow sticking almost straight up, portholes glistening. The coast guard were back to spinning the line out from the drum. The fragment of bow crested a wave, to disappear into the trough beyond. We never saw it again, just tossed debris—a hatch cover and what looked like cockpit cushions. Moments later there was oil, too, iridescent on the upslope of a swell. From the drum a line gone slack twisted down over rocks. When this was reeled in the rescue harness didn't come with it.

As instructed, we followed the police car in the Avenger, bumping down over the track to Lamlash, Jeff beside me saying nothing. When we reached smooth tarmac I broke the silence.

"I'm bloody sorry about your boat."

"I won't go into mourning for it." A moment later he added, "You'll be thinking about a new widow?"

I didn't rise to that. We took the turning up past the golf course, the white car only fifty yards ahead.

"That cruiser would have stood up to anything if he'd kept her at sea," Jeff said. "Steel hull. Why the hell didn't he?"

I knew the answer. There comes a moment out in hurricane-force weather when panic swells up to swamp reason. You can think of only one thing—shelter. Hodson had seen that shelter behind him, in the lee of Arran. He would probably have made it all right if the wind hadn't changed.

"Stokouros wasn't on board," Jeff said.

My co-director in Singapore can sometimes read what's in my mind like this. I keep refusing her proposals of marriage.

"And she has the picture," I said.

"How the hell did she persuade those two to take the boat out into that sea?"

"She was boss. And they wanted a decoy. She knew we would go to the police. That meant all the heat on the boat, none on her."

"Hodson and Kennet would play along with that? They must have known they'd be picked up. And arrested."

"What's an arrest for having got drunk at a party and stolen a boat after it? Kennet was a local boy, or almost. He'd probably have got off with a fine and a lecture from the sheriff on the evils of boozing."

"While Stokouros sneaked off Arran with the picture?"

"Yes."

A moment later he said, "Stokouros must be counting on us not doing much talking to the police."

"Do you want to tell them the truth?"

This time I could read his mind. We were becoming psychic complements fast. He was thinking about his wife up at Crinan.

"No," he said.

That was something settled. On top of the hill behind Brodick he had a question.

"What *do* we tell them?"

"It's actually what *you* tell them. I'm not really involved in this. It was your boat. I'd suggest that we had quite an alcoholic night on board; until morning, in fact. But when you were rowing me back to land you fell in. I thought you were suffering from shock and took you back to my hotel."

"An intelligent policeman could spring a few leaks in that."

186

"It's up to you to see that he doesn't."

The heater going full blast had more or less dried us off, but there hadn't been time for my clothes to take Jeff's shape and he had a crumpled look. The sergeant in the car ahead kept looking back at us through a rear window. He didn't have a kind face.

"The wind's dropping," I said.

"Big news."

I followed the Ford into a side street, braking in front of a modest-sized cement pile from which law and order is enforced on Arran for eleven and a half months in the year. For the other two weeks, during the Glasgow Fair holidays, everyone just takes cover from hordes of invaders with flick knives. The white car stopped long enough to let out the sergeant and the boy from the Hebrides, then moved around to the back of the building. Jeff was picking at my mind again.

"If you're not wanted as a corroborative witness, you plan to go Stokouros-hunting?"

"Yes."

"How do you think you'll find her?"

"Instinct."

He opened the door and joined his escort. The policemen still looked neat in damp uniforms. Jeff didn't. I watched them go up steps to disappear, then did a good-citizen wait for ten minutes in case I was needed, after which I drove down to the esplanade. The proprietor of the Italian shop was getting ready for another highly successful day in the kind of climatic conditions which ruled out beach picnics and long walks, putting most of the visitors inside his café.

"I'm not interested in your espresso coffee," I said. "Can you give me a pot of the real stuff, two fried eggs and six rashers of bacon?"

"Sure thing."

"Toast, too?"

"Okay."

He deserved to be rich. Before I ate I had a thought for Jeff, probably as hungry as I was. If he was lucky the law would provide him with a cup of tea and a digestive biscuit.

The green Mini had been returned to Tigh-na-Claddach, parked under a storm-tattered privet hedge. It was unlocked, the keys in the ignition, nothing interesting inside. By the front door the threatened climber rose was now flat down on gravel.

There was no answer to my ring, or knocking. I walked around to the French windows, to find them fastened and no one using the sitting room. The back door was also locked, the sound of my feet on cement rousing Rufus to a belated barking. If Anne was inside, she was upstairs and not receiving.

Eloise's bungalow had the curtains back. The last time I had seen it they had been drawn. From the porch I could make out the glow of an electric heater. Seated in an old lady's chair to one side of a painting after Renoir was Miss Lilias Stokouros, eating baked beans. She had a fork in one hand, a cracker in the other, the plate on her knees, and she didn't stop chewing when she looked up.

"Are you a squatter or have you permission?"

She swallowed, loading her fork again.

"Guest."

"Where's Anne Kennet?"

"Still in shock, I expect. I told her about her husband."

"How did you know?"

"I was watching. From the top of a hill above you. Through binoculars."

"You sent Angus to his death."

"I did nothing of the sort. If you want to be useful you can make some coffee."

"You're a cool bitch."

"It comes from long training."

She finished the cracker, crunching it down.

"I'm collecting the Renoir," I said.

She pointed up with her fork. "You can have that."

"It doesn't interest me. I'm talking about the picture Lady Eloise wants to sell."

"You can't have that, I'm afraid. At least, not in prime condition. And divers are expensive. Would it be worth it, even if we could get a salvage team on the job in a hurry? I don't think so."

"You want me to believe the Renoir was on that boat?"

"You can believe what you like. It was. Wrapped in a blanket. Not even protected by that suitcase you inspected. That might have given it a chance. As things are, I can't see much hope, especially if the bottom was torn out of the boat. And I'm sure you saw that oil. It's easy to imagine what is happening now. A hundred-year-old canvas and tidal movement over rocks, scraping away at it. Even if it floats the disintegration will be complete. A pity. It was an interesting work. Particularly from that connection with 'La Galette.' "

"A good act, Miss Stokouros, but it isn't quite coming across. You have that painting."

"When I've finished these beans I'm quite willing to be subjected to any reasonable search. But that suitcase over by the door isn't the right shape for Renoir-carrying, even without the frame. And if you think I've left a valuable oil under a bush somewhere in this weather, or took time off to find a cave, then you don't give me credit for much sensibility to delicate works of art. I'm very sensitive in that area."

"You left it with Anne Kennet in the main house."

"It would be my guess that Mrs. Kennet is right now mourning the loss of a Renoir as much, if not more, than the loss of a husband. But don't let me stop you from going over to hunt."

"I can't see you letting Angus take that painting out into that sea."

"I had no choice, Mr. Harris. The picture represented his future. He didn't trust us. Possibly as the result of the check I gave his wife. It was postdated to two weeks from now. She didn't like that much, either. She wrapped up her picture and took it home again."

"But why postdate your check?"

"Because everything I buy for my principals has to pass a second opinion. I'm good at assessing originals from clever fakes, but not nearly as good as a man in Rome who does a great deal of work for us. If he says yes, the payment goes through; no sees the check canceled through the head office. A sensible precaution, but Mr. Kennet wouldn't see it that way. He said that if his picture had to go to Rome he would go with it. He would hand it over when he saw the money on a table in front of him. In cash. Are you going to make that coffee?"

"No."

She got up and, taking the plate with her, went into the kitchenette. I heard her filling a kettle, then the pop of bottled gas. She called out suddenly:

"I can guess what you're thinking. That I ordered those two to sea. I had a much simpler suggestion, simply that we tie the boat up and leave it. In the circumstances I didn't think your friend would bring an action against me for borrowing his boat. All we had to do, really, was carry the Renoir back here and hang it up on its hook, which would have left you with nothing to get excited about."

I went to the door of the kitchenette. "Are you saying you wanted out of this deal?"

"Yes. It was becoming far too hot. I have plenty of other opportunities."

She put coffee powder into a cup.

"Then why did those two take the cruiser?"

"They each had their own reasons. When Kennet saw I was ready to wash my hands of the whole business, he said he would get the picture to Rome by himself. And I could meet him there. It was wild talk, but he'd screwed himself up to this one big action. He couldn't face the idea of backing out. It meant no future."

"But he must have known the police would pick up the boat."

"Not according to him. He was going to make for the west coast of Ireland."

"Hodson was ready to go to Ireland, too?"

"He wanted to. He's haunted by the idea that his former employers are stalking him. I made the mistake of saying I thought your friend was from Harwell-Speed. Am I right?"

"Yes."

She laughed. "That's going to be a nasty shock to the poor man when he comes round."

"He may have come round by now."

"No. I phoned the hospital on my way here. They suspect concussion. I'll be at his bedside when he comes back into the world."

"So will the police."

"I don't think so, Mr. Harris. I'm going to make my confession to them shortly. A worried girl who came away with Hodson for a dirty two days on Arran. And is terrified it will get into the papers and Daddy will throw her out without an allowance. The police are considerate in cases of this kind. They bend over backward not to ruin a young life. We'd had quite a party in that trailer—all those bottles, remember? Kennet talked about a boat he had the use of when he wanted, bragging about being able to do anything in a boat in any weather. But when we got out in that sea I was scared silly. Kennet went right on drinking. I finally got them to put me ashore in Brodick."

She sipped her coffee, looking at me over the cup.

"The police are going to find out that Angus had rented that trailer."

She shook her head. "They won't find that out, because he didn't. It was his. He brought it over from his garage a long time ago. For summer fun with holiday girls. His home life got him down a bit. I expect the police know all about that."

"Does Anne?"

"I didn't tell her. Maybe island gossip has. Sure you wouldn't like a cup? No? Where's your friend from Harwell-Speed?"

"I left him with the police. Making his report."

"Oh. I hope you warned him not to mention me. But he wouldn't. He's married, isn't he? He has that look. You don't. Do you ever visit Beirut?"

"Never."

The door to the porch banged in the wind. We both turned to look toward the living room as someone crossed it. For seconds I didn't recognize Anne. She was wearing a man's raincoat and had a man's tweed cap pulled on her head, all her hair shoved up under it. We watched her stretch up for the picture over the fireplace, then set this against the stone mantel. She picked up a poker and jabbed it through the canvas. She made at least seven big holes through the painting, but that wasn't enough; the top of the frame got it next, chips of gilt flying about like sparks. Then the poker dropped with a clatter onto the hearth and Anne turned slowly, seeing us.

She sat down in Eloise's chair and put her hands over her face exactly as I had seen her do behind the wheel of a Mini.

TWELVE

Lilias Stokouros stood sipping coffee, establishing a strict neutrality in whatever might be coming. I didn't want to claim a role in this piece either; the picture-wrecking had been ham melodrama. Anne was now sitting humped over, hands still up, like an actress who not only has forgotten her lines but now realizes she has no vocation for the trade. If there was some kind of symbolism, conscious or unconscious, in that old cap and raincoat belonging to Angus, my only reaction was the thought that a dedicated gardener in this climate was bound to have easy access to her own hat and coat.

Someone had to do something. I went through the door into the sitting room. Anne heard my step and looked up.

"I'm going to tell her," she said.

"Your mother?"

She nodded.

"Not much else you can do now you've made a sieve of that copy."

I hadn't meant to make that sound as rough as it did. She began to cry, a quiet sobbing like something from a little girl left all alone in one of the desolations of childhood. She sat bolt upright, only her head bent, nothing fragile about a figure swathed in rubberized fabric with long, trousered legs thrust out, largish hands on her knees. The feeling I got then was that the arrival of the adult meant to fill this body had somehow been delayed, probably was now canceled for good. If love is nurturing a set of illusions about the beloved, then that wasn't what I was suffering from, but I still wanted to provide this woman with the kind of high-walled garden which she could cultivate for the rest of her life. Only not roses from now on, none of those heat-blighted bushes that expatriates water endlessly and protect from the sun, but the local exotics, beds of cannas and jungle orchids flourishing in carefully placed rotting tree trunks. It would be a very hot garden, breathless at midday, but she would like that.

"I'm sorry about Angus," I said, stiffly conventional.

She shook her head, rejecting the sentiment or even the importance of Angus's death; I couldn't know. She got up, pushing herself by the arms of the chair, standing for a moment, then half running toward the door to the porch and out. I went onto the veranda. Anne hadn't used the path, but had gone blundering straight down over rocks to the lawn, almost losing balance as she hit its softness, but keeping her feet, starting to run again. Then she switched to an amble on a course with no obvious objective, half toward the sea.

Lilias spoke from beside me, acid. "Suicidal, would you say?"

"Shut up!"

I went after Anne. The rain had started again, but with almost no wind driving it, gentle, a mock healer bringing soothing damp to ruin. It wasn't easy to hurry on that spongy stuff underfoot and I didn't come up behind her until she had almost reached the shoreline above the sea. I took her arm.

"I'm sorry," she said, without looking at me.

"About what?"

"Just now. I've never done anything like that before. I've heard people talk about it. But I couldn't imagine it happening to me. Or how it could happen."

"How what could happen, Anne?"

"Temporary insanity, I guess you'd call it."

I didn't say anything.

"I could see what I was doing, but I couldn't stop. It was . . . as if I was taken over. It's a terrible feeling."

"Yes."

"Do you know?"

"I can guess."

We began to walk again, this time toward the rose beds and the house beyond them. I was thinking about calling the doctor, but first settling her in a chair. There was no hint of tears now; the child had gone. She seemed curious about herself, like someone who has just been told she has a serious illness, sharply alert for its symptoms.

"My poor roses. And this will have wrecked the perennial borders. I won't look until tomorrow. I'm a coward."

Ahead was an open front door. Our feet crunched on gravel getting to it, then echoed from hardwood floors on the way to the sitting room.

"I've let the fire out again."

"Sit down, Anne. I'll get you a whisky."

"The bottle's empty. I did that, too."

"Have you another?"

"Only brandy. In that cupboard. Bottom shelf."

She was perfectly calm, watching me while I poured. "You think I'm a criminal? Planning to steal that picture?"

"You're certainly a liar."

"And not very good at it?"

"I've been up against better."

"That picture really belonged to me. Morally, that is."

I took over a glass. "How do you bring morals into this?"

"Sir John Martin-Macintosh was my father."

"By blood, not adoptive?"

"By blood."

"You have proof?"

"Plenty."

She sipped, watching me. I felt like a drink myself, but not brandy.

"Who was your mother?"

"The wife of one of my father's assistants in Malaya."

"Did your father's assistant know you weren't his daughter?"

"He died two months before I was born. From a gun accident on a jungle tour. I'm pretty sure he knew."

"You're suggesting he shot himself just before the end of his wife's pregnancy?"

"Well, it was over thirty years ago. They cared a lot more about personal honor and that sort of thing in those days."

I stood in front of the dead fire, looking down at Anne. Without being in any position to pass judgments, I still wondered just what the proportion of fabrication to fact were in this mix.

"Have you ever met your real mother?"

"No. She died in Brighton last year. She'd married again."

"How long have you known this about your parents?"

"Since I was eleven. I was flying home after the holidays in Malaya, with another girl. Going back to school. She told me. Just after we'd taken off from Bangkok. I remember that. I also remember that we were drinking Cokes. My friend seemed to find my parentage much more exciting than her own."

"So the fact that you were Sir John's daughter was local gossip in Malaya then?"

"It must have been."

"The next time you saw your father did you ask him about this?"

"No." Anne drank. "I told you, I'm a coward."

"Now you have proof. What is it?"

"Father told me three months before he died. He said he loved my mother still. When I was born he had wanted a divorce from Eloise to marry my mother, in spite of what this would have done to his career. Eloise wouldn't have any of that.

She took me instead. On condition that my mother didn't see me again, or try to."

"Your real mother never did?"

Anne shook her head.

"You've never told Lady Eloise that you know who your father was?"

"Not openly. She knows I know, of course. But if I tried to talk about it she'd just flatly deny it. She never admits anything that doesn't fit in with her planning. Deliberately doesn't see it. My father leaving her was something she didn't see, either. She had plans for him; he was to become governor of somewhere important. I think she wanted Hong Kong. Tetuan was a big disappointment. Maybe I had something to do with that. The gossip. But I don't think Father ever really rated a top governorship, even with Eloise's whip behind him. You can make me talk, Paul. It's as though you have a right to the answers. But you don't!"

Her voice was much louder.

"No, I don't. You can switch off if you want."

"I don't want to, damn you!"

I sat down, resigning as prosecutor, but she didn't much like the waiting. It could have been that she didn't like the silence in the house around us, something she was going to have to learn to live with if she stayed here. The threat of those silences from being solitary can make bloody fools of us all.

"Paul, what do you think happened to that picture? I mean is it ruined?"

"Our art expert over in the bungalow has written it off."

"I see. It's Angus I should be thinking of, isn't it? Not pictures?"

"No. I hate phony grief. I burned my black tie years ago."

"I loved him once!"

"Let's leave out that section of your confessions, shall we?"

"I *hate* you!"

"Sure."

"Why did you come?"

"I thought Miss Stokouros still had the Renoir."

Suddenly she leaned forward in her chair. "You've been married. What happened to your wife?"

"She killed herself driving a car. It was probably intentional."

"I'm not surprised!"

"I was. I thought I'd been a model husband."

"The bastards always do!"

In anger she scored quite well, aiming with an intuitive feel for the area of weakness. All I could do was bat back at once, but was knocked off my stroke by a stab from the pain that can still come when a scar is bumped.

"Who commissioned that imitation Renoir to fool an old woman? You or Angus?"

"Hodson said he would have it done and let us see it, that's all. He'd taken color photographs. But we neither of us . . ."

"You were to decide when you saw the copy? Whether it was good enough? If it was it might have been months before your mother realized that anything was wrong. You knew that she didn't look at it all that often, for all she talked about it. My sudden arrival caught you all out. You signaled Hodson to get here quick with the fake. He did more than that; he brought his client."

There was a crash of glass against brickwork, then a faint hissing from still-hot ash. Anne was on her feet, walking over toward the long windows as though she meant to escape through them. I shouted, "You knew that Angus had tampered with that chair. You knew he was on the island. You suspected that he had chopped your mother into the rose bed."

She spun around. "No! That's not true! I met him at the ferry—"

"Did you see him get off the boat?"

Anger seemed to drain out of her. "Paul, I didn't *know*. I swear it! I didn't! All right, I may have been suspicious. But if

198

he was on Arran he didn't stay here. He must have slept in his trailer. He did that often enough."

She was bitter. She came back to a chair and sat in it.

"I started everything; I admit that. I mean when Hodson suggested we might sell the picture without mother knowing. But Angus took over. He went wild on it. He saw the money, nothing else."

"You weren't looking at the money?"

"Oh, God! You won't listen to me. Of course I wanted it. Because I had a right to it. The picture was mine! It belonged to my family, to me, through my father. It had nothing to do with Eloise. She—"

"She was his wife."

"His slave driver!"

"Convenient for you to believe that. Maybe he wanted to be governor. Most men would in his circumstances. And Eloise found the money to help him. From her own work. Don't forget that."

"As if I could forget it! Or she would ever let him forget it."

"So you knew she was E. Kell?"

"Yes. Father told me. When he told me about my mother. It was a kind of explanation of why he'd had to stay with Eloise."

"But he didn't know about the Renoir?"

She shook her head. "I don't think so."

"Why did you take the Renoir to the trailer? Without Angus?"

"Because the choice had to be mine."

"You mean you wanted to compare the real with the fake, to see if the fake would work?"

"No! I had to decide whether to sell or not to sell. And I decided not to, because I couldn't. Even though I had a right to do it, I couldn't sell that picture."

"If you weren't going to sell, why bring the fake back here? To show Angus that the fake wasn't good enough?"

"No!"

"I think the answer is yes. That you had very cold feet on the whole business. Because I'd shown up and was ready to take Lady Eloise to London. There was too much risk suddenly. Angus could face that risk but you couldn't. That's what you fought about. Then he just walked out, taking the Renoir with him, leaving you scared silly."

Anne didn't move, letting silence come back. It was almost as if an audience had gone still for the big climax, no noise at all, no one coughing, just a breathing that spread through open doors, from room to room. But there was no big climax; she just said softly:

"What's the use?"

I didn't know then what I had been trying to do. Perhaps it was to build up some kind of basic honesty between us that we could both stand on even if it meant falsehoods all around us for the world. But she was right, it was no use. I got up.

"Can I make a suggestion?" I said. "Don't tell Lady Eloise about your part in what has happened. Angus can take the blame. You knew nothing about what he was up to."

She stared. "You think I could live with that?"

"We all live with a skeleton somewhere."

"I won't do it!"

"Don't be a fool. Why make yourself a target for Eloise's fury?"

"I deserve it."

"When you've recovered from this attack of conscience I think you'll see sense."

"All you feel for me is contempt."

"No. Want to know what I'm feeling right now?"

She gave absolutely no sign that she did, so after waiting for all of half a minute I turned and went out. Sitting in my car out in the drive, I remembered lines from the Japanese translated by Arthur Waley. They weren't exactly bang on to my situation, but they had a certain relevance.

How can one e'er be sure
That true love will endure?
My thoughts this morning are
As tangled as my hair.

Anne and I hadn't even had the tangled hair.

A girl on the pumps at Macdonald's garage in Brodick indicated a large shed with open doors. Inside this a pair of legs stuck out from under a battered station wagon.

"Mr. Macdonald?"

A voice said, "He's been buried twenty-one years."

"Are you the new owner?"

"Aye. What was you wantin'?"

"A gearbox."

"What make of car?"

"A Land-Rover."

The legs started to wiggle. The man who emerged in overalls black and stiff with grease was about forty and on the short side when he had pulled himself up. He had lost his hair and his illusions. Pale-blue eyes with heavy red veining were the kind the whisky companies never picture in their advertising.

"Is it your Land-Rover?"

"Major Henderson-Pratt's."

"He sent you here? To chivvy me up, like?"

"No. I was with him when he stripped everything except top."

"Aye, well, top's gone now, too. She's a load of junk out the back."

"Could you put her on the road again with a new box?"

"Maybe. But what's it to you?"

"I'll pay for it."

"You his brother?"

I didn't care for that at all.

"No relation. Just a friend."

"Wish I had friends who'd pay my bills."

"Could you get a new box from the mainland, fast?"

"No fast, but I could get it. The major's been on to me about a reconditioned box. I keep telling him he hasnae a hope in hell. And I'll tell *you* something, mister, if you was with him when that old crock packed in. You was both poaching up there on that loch. The major hasnae any fishing rights on this island."

"We didn't catch anything."

"That's nae surprise to me. I could guddle a fish with my two hands afore he could catch one. You know what a new Land-Rover box'll cost you?"

"Plenty."

"Aye, well, it's no for me to say you're daft. Does the major know about this?"

"No."

"So what'll I say when he asks me where I got a new box from?"

"I don't think he will ask."

The man stared at me. "You'll pay by check? In advance?" I nodded.

"I'll have to see your credits. Come over to the office."

Jeff's style demanded a backing of the good things: cabin cruisers with flying bridges, a Jaguar at least, probably a Jensen, and at home the right bits of Sheraton scattered around. I was sure his wife was beautiful. Seated on an esplanade bench in Brodick under a gray sky with a chill wind blowing, he might have been a refugee from the collapse of capitalism. My clothes didn't help. He looked at me without pleasure.

"I expected to see you with a Renoir under your arm. You haven't met up with Stokouros?"

"I met up with her. She hasn't got it."

"Then where the hell is it?"

I told him. He minded, but I think he would have minded

more if he had seen the picture, his pain at its loss now conditioned by a natural skepticism born of long experience where alleged works of art were concerned.

"So it's back to square one, except that I haven't got a boat?"

"Just about. The police didn't bring out the thumbscrews?"

"That sergeant would have enjoyed doing it. Your watertight story kept springing leaks."

"Why?"

"He kept asking me to time things. Like when we stopped drinking. Was it five A.M. when I rowed you ashore and had my accident? Or six? It does me no good in these parts to be known as an all-night boozer. I live here. I'm thinking of standing for the county council. Also, he wanted a deep analysis of my relationship with you. I wasn't awfully good at that either."

"What did you tell him?"

"Practically that we'd gone to nursery school together. That man's suspicious. All Highlanders are suspicious, but the sergeant twice as much as most. I think he wants promotion to the mainland."

"He hasn't a thing against us."

"Not until some seaweed gatherer picks up a tattered painting on a beach and an old lady resident starts shouting that it's her Renoir. That'll see a file reopened."

"One of the coast guard told me that the currents around here take everything to Ireland. I think you need a drink."

"I think so, too," Jeff said.

We went into the hotel with chandeliers, where they had a look at us and considered invoking that clause about the management declining to admit patrons not wearing neckties, but we got into the cocktail bar, which was just open for the pre-lunch trade and already starting to fill with people sour about the prevailing climatic conditions. I bought two rounds quite fast and when dampened by a second whisky, Jeff's mustache began to look almost normal. He told me he was going home that afternoon, his wife coming down to meet the small ferry from Lochranza. He didn't think she was going to care too much for our story to the police about the loss of his boat, and he had been sitting on that bench trying to think up a better one, his mind blank.

"You won't get on the Ardrossan ferry today, if that's what you're planning," Jeff said. "I can push two wheels anywhere, but all these people in here are just panting to get home. Mass evacuation. Any breakdown in contemporary communications starts a panic."

I bought him lunch, fresh salmon and a reasonable hock. He ate and drank with relish, but still couldn't love me, so I made a play for his commercial side.

"Jeff, if the art-selling business in the West is suffering from the recession, why not set up a branch out East?"

He didn't look interested. "Sounds like a good way to lose money."

"I don't think you would. We're doing all right. Good rubber and tin prices. And with oil all around us, we can do without the Arabs. We've got people still looking for sound investments."

"So have we. Only they're not finding any."

"Buying art with a view to future profit would certainly seem a novel idea to most of my business associates. But you can sell anything with the right promotion. I'm still getting maximum output absorption for a diesel engine that came off the drawing boards twenty years ago."

"You're too mean to retool your factory?"

"Why should I? It's cheaper to advertise."

He emptied his wineglass and I refilled it.

"Harwell-Speed in Singapore? I don't think so."

"Then you won't mind if I put up the idea to Sotheby's on my way through London?"

"*What?*"

"Whoever gets to Singapore first could have an absolute stranglehold in the Ming and Tang trade before their rivals got wise to a new opportunity. It's at least worth a preliminary survey. Conducted by you."

"Is it?"

"I have an apartment with two bedrooms and two baths, which means only your air fare, no hotel expenses."

"That would certainly appeal to the rest of our directors." He wiped mayonnaise from his mustache. "I know why you've come up with this, Paul. Last-minute bid to save a potentially beautiful friendship from sudden death."

"That's right."

He began to laugh.

Aishah still wasn't looking at the customers, though she was decked out this evening like a package-holiday ad for a ration of the good life under palm trees, wearing her brightest things, a surprising color mix. I was served my drink and issued my change without any eye contact between us and was talking to the Seychellian émigré when George came in from the hall carrying a case of bottled stout. Aishah looked at him and he put down his load and looked at her. It only lasted seconds but during them the muted gush of music from the tape wasn't even remotely adequate; there should have been a sudden swelling of violins.

It's not often easy to guess what has started to make a dead marriage tick again, but in this case I could. Aishah had received that supreme accolade from a caring husband; what she did was still important enough to make him shoot at her twice. A decaying pig doesn't get himself worked up to anything like that degree of commitment, but the lover goes amok with passion, and if they both survive, youth is miraculously given back to them. I had been the catalyst, these two owed me a good deal, but I didn't expect to get any credit for it.

All around the bar Angus Kennet was being given a one-night tribute of everyone's interest, though I didn't see faces registering anything approaching real shock. The dead man had only earned the status of an out-of-town member here, not seen often, and when he did show up, never really becoming one of the boys. As the Seychellian suggested, not being a clubman must have worked against him out East, where a low handicap isn't enough; you have to be a real success with a glass in your hand at the nineteenth hole, too, otherwise it's the handshake and you're out.

Hendy arrived late, looking parboiled, which rather spoiled the solemn effect of his advance down the long room. He explained that he'd had to come on his bike, which was why he was a bit short of wind and thought he'd better have a whisky first. As the golf partner of the deceased, his category tonight was special and there was a glass in his hand almost at once as well as a crowd around him. I stood up at the bar, looking at Aishah's back as she polished glasses; it was remarkable how she contrived to move her whole body over a relatively simple job that most people would just use hands for. I didn't see Hendy approaching me, just heard this evening's obituary tones.

"Terrible business, Harris, isn't it?"

"Yes."

"I tried to phone Tigh-na-Claddach. To see if there was anything I could do to help. Couldn't get through. Must be disconnected."

"Probably."

"That poor girl. First her mother, then this. I must say I can't understand Angus taking that boat. He wasn't the sort who showed his drink. I mean, going wild or anything."

"Oh."

"I wonder if Mrs. Kennet will stay on at Tigh-na-Claddach. Bit lonely for her now. I don't think she makes friends easily. She didn't seem to get on with my wife. Did you get the impression, Harris, that she prefers men?"

"Yes."

"Bit awkward, really, isn't it? I mean I can't just sort of pop up there now that Angus has gone. You've no idea how gossip whizzes about this island. And one has to watch it."

"I'm sure."

There were a couple of wet beer rings on the counter which Aishah hadn't mopped away. I stared at them.

"You know, aside from this tragedy it's been quite a good day for me in a way. I mean I've had a stroke of luck. More than that, really. I know I've groused to you about this place, wondering if the wife and I made a mistake coming here. But now I know we didn't. Stay long enough, and don't do anything to upset them, and they take you in."

"Who?"

"The locals. I mean the island people."

"Become established as an Arran resident, have you?"

"It certainly looks like it. You know what my garage man has done? Gone to the trouble of phoning round scrapyards on the mainland until he found one that was breaking up a Land-Rover. The unbelievable thing is that the gearbox was all right. Practically as good as new. All I'm going to have to pay is a few pounds plus the fitting charges. I don't mind telling you that the thought of the bill for all this was sending me up the wall. Tight budget and all that. But can you imagine any city garage doing something like this for a customer these days?"

"No, I can't really."

"To me it's all the difference between having transport and none at all. The wife can't ride a bike. We wouldn't have got into Brodick to shop. What I'm saying is . . . sudden kindness, you know. It just makes you feel you're home."

I was still looking at the beer stains, not liking what I had to do.

"Had you fixed up to play any golf with Kennet?"

Hendy seemed surprised. "Yes. He rang me to fix this week-end."

"When did he ring?"

"What? Oh, that morning we were going fishing, I think it was. Yes, that's right."

"He called you from his mainland garage?"

"I suppose so. No, wait a minute—I seem to remember it was a call box. He had to press a button for the connection. What are you getting at?"

I looked around. No one seemed interested in us. Aishah was at the other end of the bar, drawing beer.

"Did you tell him we were going fishing?"

"I think I may have. Why are you asking me questions? Is there . . . something queer about this Kennet business? You know, I've wondered. After that night at Tigh-na-Claddach, when I saw—"

"I don't want to hear about what you saw, Major. I want you to forget all about that night. And don't develop any theories you might have here in this bar, now or later."

"What? That sounds as though you were—"

"I'm just asking you to forget, that's all. For the sake of a widow."

He stared. "Asking me? You're not *asking* me!" There was a moment's silence. When he spoke again, it wasn't much more than a whisper. "That gearbox . . ."

He was a lot brighter than he looked.

"Let's have another whisky," I suggested.

If I had really been playing fairy godfather to Hendy, I might have slept better than I did. I phoned the hospital before breakfast. The matron told me that Lady Eloise was traveling in an ambulance on the late-afternoon ferry for an operation to her hip in Glasgow, and not only was there every chance she would survive, but she would be able to walk as well as she had done before the accident, if not better. Mrs. Kennet had seen her mother the night before and was due in at ten this morning. Lady Eloise had been asking to see me and the rules about visiting hours would be waived for my appointment with the patient at eleven.

While I was driving toward Brodick the weather gods, by a narrow majority vote, decided that it was time to give Arran another spell of the Mediterranean. Goat Fell was back to playing at being a long-extinct tropic volcano nursing lush growth on lava ash. The Clyde estuary had switched on a glittering blue that seemed lit from underwater, and a flock of colored sails spattered the horizon near one of the mainland towns, probably a storm-postponed regatta, the men out there playing hooky from their Glasgow offices to crew boats. One of the few remaining cargo-passenger liners was coming downriver with its departure flags flying, bound for South America, or the Orient, giving me a couple of sharp pricks of longing to be on her.

It was only twenty-five past ten when I reached the hospital compound with the idea of parking beside a green Mini, waiting for Anne to come out, but I hadn't put a scrambler on my thoughts and she picked them up. The Mini was starting down the drive as I started up it; I could hear the bluebottle buzzing of that little box accelerating. The roadway was just wide enough for two cars to pass, flanked on my side by bushes, and on the Mini's by a bed of variegated snapdragons regimented into a square space as tightly as National Health outpatients waiting to see a specialist. I did what you do when you want to stop an approaching car—braked and swung the Avenger over toward the snapdragons, leaving the Mini not much more than two feet of asphalt.

We saw each other very distinctly. I don't know how I was looking, but she was looking determined, a girl who is quite sure where she is going, her route on the journey in no way destined to parallel mine. The Mini didn't slacken speed, it just swerved up over a narrow grass border, and then, bringing Armageddon to the snapdragons, sliced off blooms, to be thrown up on a stubby hood, together with clods of soft earth. For a moment I thought the little car was going to bog down, but it churned its way out, two wheels still retaining traction, the exhaust snorting. I saw the side of her face as she went past me, then blond hair was a screen as she leaned forward over a gear change.

I could have given chase, but a mangled bed of flowers told me how much good that would do, so I just watched the Mini through the gates, then drove on to the car park, to sit staring at tarmac steaming under sun, with the building beyond offering the mystery that encapsulates all hospitals, tidying away pain into a neat containment behind stone and concrete. What I was feeling required another kind of containment.

At two minutes past eleven I walked down a hospital corridor with the matron.

"Lady Martin-Macintosh really shouldn't be having two visitors so close together, Mr. Harris. Last night, after she'd been given the news of Mr. Kennet's death, extra sedation was necessary. I can only let you have fifteen minutes. We've put her in a private room."

She opened a door.

Eloise had her curlers in; Anne must have brought them. Dresden china, damaged but repairable, was propped up on about six pillows. If she was still under sedation, this hadn't muzzed her mental processes. As soon as the door shut and I was in a chair over to the right of the bed, the big guns were opened on Angus, and with no respect for the dead. He was a murderer and a wicked thief on top of being a commercial failure. There wasn't even light ack-ack fire toward Anne, which told me pretty plainly that an adopted daughter had done as I suggested and kept herself a nontarget by avoiding the whole truth and nothing but the truth. You can give advice which you aren't really too happy to have taken, and perhaps that was my reaction. At the same time it made sense for Anne to have covered herself if she meant to go on living with this old woman. I had no doubts, even before Eloise confirmed this, that Anne was now planning to do exactly that.

At least seven of our fifteen minutes were taken up by Angus and a lost Renoir that would have fetched that highly inflated price of a quarter of a million, according to Eloise, and I daresay if you owned a picture that was actually worth only a fifth of that round sum, and had an evil son-in-law as well, seven minutes isn't too long to devote to the loss of both. But it seemed long to me, and I switched to that low-geared assumption of interest, with nods at intervals, which builds you up as a sympathetic listener. It wasn't until Eloise had blown off a full head of steam that I really said anything at all.

"I hear you have to have an operation?"

"Yes."

Operations weren't important; if you have sense and determination you survive them, and Eloise had both. She had quite some living to do yet and meant to do it in her own way, hospitalization merely an interlude to be endured. I had been fully reinstated as the son of my dear father, my mother forgotten. When I wasn't looking at Eloise's rage-marked face, which by some miracle still had the porcelain uncracked, I looked at a bunch of flowers and a half-empty bottle of orangeade. Suddenly she really startled me.

"I hope they don't find the body!"

"What?"

"I don't want Anne troubled by a funeral. After what she has been through. And he certainly doesn't deserve a *Christian* burial!"

I didn't say anything. Eloise didn't notice.

"Anne needs a complete change of scene. As soon as I'm ready to travel we'll go."

"Where?"

"Ooty, of course."

This was quite a surprise. Without the Renoir I had thought there simply wouldn't be the finance for the Ootacamund project.

"Paul, do you ever feel that you have been guided?"

I considered this. To be guided implied God somewhere in

the scheme, which I would have thought out of character for Eloise. But maybe not. Her God would be a personal convenience.

"In the sense that you mean," I said carefully, "I can't say that it has been part of my experience."

"That's because you resist. You don't believe in signs?"

"Not all that much."

"Light me a cigarette."

It was probably forbidden in the hospital, but she had a packet in her handbag. Crippled fingers took my offering.

"Yesterday the first thing I did was ask to see the papers. I always read the papers. Do you?"

"I'm quite glad to skip them sometimes."

"I can never sleep unless I've read the day's papers."

She let out a deep inhalation of the smoke which after all these years should have seen her with emphysema at the very least, but hadn't, then pointed.

"Down there."

A bent forefinger indicated newsprint stuffed into a shelf under the flowers and the orange drink. I pulled out a financial section and was about to unfold it when she said:

"No, don't bother. It's just that advertisement. The one about annuities. Read it."

Bold black print invited those with capital and of a retirement age to secure the future against inflation with a graduated annuity pension for life. By accepting a smaller interest rate at the start, you allowed your income to increase by seven percent each year until you died. Listed were the returns you could expect for a straight annuity on your own life according to your age when you handed over your capital. Sore fingers had nonetheless been able to make a little pencil tick opposite the interest rate for Eloise's age, in her case fifteen percent at the start. A rather too long silence from me must have irritated her.

"Well, Paul?"

I looked up.

"It seems quite a good idea on the face of it," I said. "Except hat current inflation rates around the world are anywhere rom fifteen percent up."

"*Not* in Ooty."

"You think seven percent more income every year will do for ndia?"

"Certainly. I intend to sell Tigh-na-Claddach. It should be worth at least thirty thousand pounds. There is no mortgage; I own it outright. At fifteen percent on thirty thousand pounds, my income would start right away at four thousand five hundred. And go up every year after that. Do you think that's a reputable insurance company?"

"If it isn't, you can find one that is. Quite a few have these chemes."

"Well, then, don't you see? I'm all right. I don't expect one has to pay much tax in India if one's a foreigner. And if I use my money that way, I ought to have a bigger income than Mabel. I'm sure she doesn't have four thousand five hundred to ive on, or anything like it. Probably very few people in Ooty will have a bigger income than I do."

Eloise didn't actually say so, but it was obvious she believed he had been guided to see that advertisement just at a time when she thought she had lost the future she wanted. Some kinds of faith are frightening to contemplate. I sat there slightly humbed, but was suddenly prodded alert again by a startling hought. . . . Eloise, for all her protestations, had never really been dead certain that her picture *was* a Renoir. The experts n London might have said no. Even Lilias Stokouros's belief hat the picture was authentic had to be subjected to the test of that Rome verdict, and if the painting had survived there was always the chance it would turn out to be an interesting curiosity worth a few hundred. Eloise was now absolved from the hreat of this grim moment of truth which might have nicked quite badly even her reinforced-concrete ego.

"There's only one snag I can see," I said. "When you buy an annuity you spend your capital."

She seemed surprised. "What's wrong with that at my age?"

"There's no money for your heirs."

She thought about that. "You mean Anne?"

"Yes."

"Well, there'll be enough for us both to live very well in Ooty When I'm gone Anne can do what I've done."

"Buy an annuity?"

"That's right."

"What with?"

"Oh, there should be some money for that. I have a little capital as well as Tigh-na-Claddach. I'll put that aside for Anne Then there's the garage business I bought for that man. There's a loan on it, but when that's paid off there should be some money left. Quite a little nest egg, really."

It was my guess that "little" was the operative word for that nest egg. Anne, in Ootacamund, would spend years pouring tea and lighting cigarettes and taking Eloise for short walks about the garden to watch the Tamils weeding. The chances were that she would be somewhere in her forties when Eloise was finally guided out of this world, a bit late in the day for Anne to start making much of a career for herself, but still far too soon to get a decent return on an annuity. Overnight she would be a poor white in a community of aging ex-colonials, with the choice of supplementing a trickle income either by teaching English to Madrasis or by becoming the companion-help of another British terminal escaper. I can't think of many worse fates than being a poor white in the contemporary Orient. In Singapore there is a charity to which I contribute almost entirely devoted to relieving their distress.

Why in hell's name hadn't Anne seen what she was walking into, or, having seen it, put up some kind of a fight? And then I thought of what she'd had in living so far. There weren't many pointers suggesting that her experience had included much of the Eloise type of guidance, or love either.

"Paul, what's the matter with you?"

"Nothing."

"So you think this is a good idea?"

I tried to keep any viciousness out of my voice.

"For you, yes."

She remained serene.

"It's so useful having a man's advice. I miss it. Not that John was very good at business."

I waited for her to suggest that I had been guided to Arran, but maybe there was something in my face that stopped her; she didn't.

The door opened. The matron was looking at the cigarette. Eloise crushed this out in a saucer, but only because it was down to the filter.

"Oh, a few more minutes, matron. I'm feeling fine."

Perhaps there is something just slightly intimidating about having a Lady as a patient in a cottage hospital. The door closed again.

The Avenger was four cars behind the ambulance in a queue moving slowly out over the long pier toward the ferry. A highly colored sunset used Goat Fell as its main foreground prop, laying a rough-edged shadow of the mountain well out onto the waters of the firth. Brodick was back in the semiexotic holiday business, storm debris tidied away, and from this distance it looked as though the palms had already had their broken fronds nipped off. Probably up at the hospital gardeners had rushed in fresh snapdragon plants to replace the casualties, though I couldn't believe much had been done for the Tigh-na-Claddach roses, Anne being up there inside that white van with frosted windows, seeing that the patient was kept comfortable on the journey. The patient was making all the plans for their future, too. She and Anne would be going to a small hotel on Scotland's east coast for the convalescence, the money for this, and the later first-class passages to India by sea, presumably coming out of the nice little nest egg.

I watched the ambulance ease itself over the segmented steel ramp and then gently bump down into the ferry's belly. Following in my turn, I got out of the car as a vast trailer truck maneuvered into place, its diesel roaring and belching fumes. I went through a hatch to the stairs up, but on deck didn't walk around to where I could have a last look at Arran, but stood to gaze over toward the mainland, where the industrial smog hadn't yet cleared up for the day. When we landed at Ardrossan the ambulance would turn north and I would turn south. Two days from now I would be back in Singapore, checking to see whether the elderly Chinese woman who pretends to clean for me had forgotten to water the roof terrace's potted plants, which she would have done. Every time I leave home for more than a week I have to buy new plants.

The only good thing I can find to say for air travel is that by the time you have recovered from flight disorientation, you find that the door to yesterday has been automatically slammed behind you. It is as though projection through space is an analgesic to the recent past; you remember there was pain, but the hurt has become only an ache. I would take a whisky out onto a tiled patio four floors above the Singapore river, sitting down in the stink from mud at low tide, an unnerving return to emotional adolescence on a Scottish island something now well behind me and perhaps just slightly embarrassing to recall. At least that was what I was hoping for this time.

I didn't use the ship's restaurant on the crossing, just sat on a bench until the loudspeaker requested that all owners of vehicles return to them for the drive off. The Avenger was almost directly opposite the hatch into a clanging cave, but I didn't go straight to the car, walking forward to an ambulance positioned to be first off when the ramp fell. Sometimes these vehicles have a square of tinted glass you can just see through, but this one didn't, as resistant to Peeping Toms as a railway carriage lavatory. I stood by white-painted steel listening for voices, but the rumble of the ship's engines was suddenly added to by the driver of the trailer truck's test-running his diesel, and if the patient inside that sealed box had started to scream I wouldn't have heard it. I had a wild impulse to beat on the side panels, or the back door, shouting to Anne to come out while there was still time, but I didn't, just walked back down the ship.

It was then I saw the blue Audi parked at an angle out from the curve of the ferry's hull. There were two people in it, Lilias Stokouros behind the wheel, and in the seat beside her, a man wearing a white turban bandage. Both were looking at me. Lilias nodded and smiled. Maybe I should have sent a signal back, but all I did was get into the Avenger and shut the door.

The ship's engines cut out. The ramp clanged down. The ambulance left us, bouncing quite a bit on the hinged bridge this time, in a hurry. I switched on the ignition. Back in Singapore there was a Thai girl who might be quite glad to see me again, or might not, according to her mood.